*Enid Blyton*

# CLEVER-ONE THE IMP

## and other stories

# CLIVEDEN PRESS

Published in Great Britain in 1991 by Cliveden Press,
an Egmont Company, Egmont House, PO Box 111,
Great Ducie Street, Manchester M60 3BL.
Printed in the United Kingdom.
ISBN 0 7498 0410 6
1st reprint 1992

# *Enid Blyton*

Enid Blyton was born in London in 1897. Her childhood was spent in Beckenham, Kent, and as a child she began to write poems, stories and plays. She trained to be a teacher but she devoted her whole life to being a children's author. Her first book was a collection of poems for children, published in 1922. In 1926 she began to write a weekly magazine for children called *Sunny Stories*, and it was here that many of her most popular stories and characters first appeared. The magazine was immensely popular and in 1953 it became *The Enid Blyton Magazine*.

She wrote more than 600 books for children and many of her most popular series are still published all over the world. Her books have been translated into over 30 languages. Enid Blyton died in 1968.

# Contents

## *Clever-One the imp*

At one end of Tick-Tock Village lived the goblin, Gloomy. At the other end lived the witch, Greedy. In between were the cottages of the pixies, elves and imps.

"We're most unlucky," they said to one another when they met at the market each day. "If we don't meet Gloomy, with his bad temper and moans and groans, we bump into Greedy, with her horrid ways. And we don't dare to offend them because they really know more magic than we do!"

Clever-One the imp didn't know Gloomy or Greedy. He had just come to stay with his brother, Poppit, who lived near to Gloomy. He listened to everything that was said, and then he looked very thoughtful.

Poppit looked at him. "He's thinking," he said proudly to everyone. "He's thinking very hard. Soon his head will swell up and we shall know he's got a good idea."

Just then Greedy came by and pushed everyone out of the way. Then Gloomy came up, frowning and muttering, and all the little folk scurried off. But not Clever-One. He still stayed where he was, thinking. His head swelled up and Poppit, who was watching him from a good way off, knew he had suddenly got an idea.

Greedy glared at him and pushed him off the pavement. Gloomy, who was walking in the road, bumped into him, and pushed him back on to the pavement.

"What are you dreaming of?" he growled. "Standing there in everybody's way."

"Dear me, I'm so sorry," said Clever-

One, "but the truth is, I was just wondering where in the world I put the magic broomstick that belonged to my grandmother. It would be so useful just now, because my car has broken down. It's a wonderful broomstick, better than any other in the world, because it goes higher and faster."

Gloomy and Greedy stared at Clever-One and suddenly became quite polite to him. "What a wonderful broomstick!" said Witch Greedy, who only had a very ordinary one that refused to fly at all on a rainy or a windy night.

"Where *can* it be?" said Goblin Gloomy, who hadn't got a flyaway broomstick at all.

"I must find out," said Clever-One. "Yes, I really must. I'll hunt for it till I find it."

"*Do* let me know when you find it," said Greedy. "I'll buy it from you."

"No. *I'll* buy it!" said Gloomy, crossly. "She's got one already. Greedy thing!"

"I'll make your nose grow long and

then put a knot in it!" said Witch Greedy, angrily.

Goodness knows what would have happened if Clever-One hadn't walked off, still looking as if he was thinking very deeply. The goblin and the witch both followed him at once.

They kept him in sight all day and he led them a fine dance. But when night came, and all three were tired, Clever-One made his way to a lonely cave in a hill at the back of the village. Gloomy and Greedy followed him, feeling certain that the imp had remembered the place where his grandmother's broomstick was.

In the cave, sure enough, was a long, strong broomstick, with a fine sweeping-end that had never been used. "Aha!" said Clever-One, loudly. "Here it is." He took hold of it, sat on the stick and galloped round the cave with it.

Greedy and Gloomy both rushed in. They caught hold of the broomstick too.

"Sell it to me!" cried Gloomy.

"No, to me!" shouted Greedy, and they both tried to tug it away.

"Now, now, what manners!" said Clever-One, shocked. "Surely you don't want to break it between you? Now, I'll tell you what I'll do. I'll let you each have a ride on it to see if you like it before you buy it."

"No," said Greedy. "If Gloomy sits on it and rides off, he'll never come back. I know him, the deceitful rogue."

"Ho!" said Gloomy, frowning so hard that his eyes disappeared. "And what about *you*, Madam? I know perfectly well that once *you* get on it, you'll ride off through the night, and keep the stick for your own for always."

"Dear, dear!" said Clever-One, looking puzzled. "Then I daren't let either of you ride alone. I know! You can take a ride together! That will be a splendid idea."

Greedy and Gloomy looked sharply at Clever-One. "There's a trick in this!"

said Gloomy. "I smell it! You're going to send us both off somewhere on this magic broomstick of yours – and you think we'll never come back, so that the Village of Tick-Tock will be rid of us!"

"Very well," said Clever-One, looking offended. "If you think that, don't ride the broomstick. I'll have it for myself."

"No. You ride with us!" cried Greedy, and pulled Clever-One down on to the broomstick in front of her. "Get on, Gloomy. Now, if he plays any tricks with us, and sends us off to the moon, he'll go too! Ha, ha, ha!"

"Wait, wait! Let me strap my parcel on my back," said Clever-One as he picked up something from the floor. He put it over his shoulders. "I need both hands to hold the broomstick."

All three sat on the big broomstick, and walked it to the cave entrance. Clever-One suddenly struck the stick hard and cried out loudly. "To the Moon! To the Moon! And don't come back for a week, old broomstick!"

"You rogue!" cried the witch. "I thought you'd play a trick. But you'll have to come too! Ho, ho! We shall make you our servant up there for a whole week!"

Up into the air went the broomstick with a loud swishing noise like a rocket. The three held on tightly. The broomstick circled round and then went straight up towards the big round moon in the sky.

Was Clever-One frightened? Did he mind what was happening? Not a bit of it!

When they were fairly high up, just reaching the first clouds, Clever-One pulled a cord that hung down in front of him, and was attached to the parcel he carried. Then he suddenly leapt off the broomstick, with such a terrible yell that the witch and the goblin almost fell off in fright themselves.

"He's gone!" said Gloomy. "Good riddance! I hope he lands with a hard bump!"

"He'll think twice before he plays tricks on anyone again," said Greedy. "Nasty little imp! Serves him right."

But Clever-One wasn't about to hurt himself. Oh, no! The parcel he had tied to himself was a neatly folded parachute, and when he pulled the cord, and jumped off into the air, the parachute began to open! Soon it was fully open, and Clever-One began to float gently downwards to earth.

"Here I come!" he shouted to all the folk of Tick-Tock, who had heard the swishing of the broomstick and had come running out to see what was happening. "Here I come! I'm frozen. Somebody get me some hot cocoa!"

"Where are Greedy and Gloomy?" cried Poppit.

"Probably on the moon by now," said Clever-One, coming gently down to earth. "They wanted my broomstick and they got it. We won't see them for at least a week. That will teach them a lesson!"

# A tale about Tumpy

I must tell you a tale about Tumpy and his caravan. He and Mr Spells shared it with Bits the dog. It was a most unusual caravan because it had feet instead of wheels, and it could walk for miles, taking Tumpy, Mr Spells and Bits with it.

Now one day Tumpy looked at the caravan curtains and he saw that they were very dirty. "Look here, Spells," he said, "just look at these curtains! You must wash them!"

"Good gracious, no!" said Spells, alarmed. "I couldn't possibly wash big things like these. You wash them yourself!"

"Oh, well," said Tumpy, "we'll send

them to the washerwoman in the next village – what's her name now – Mrs Suds."

"All right. I'll take them down and

pack them into the basket," said Spells. "Hey, Bits – come and hold the ladder for me!" Bits the dog helped all he could. Mr Spells took down the curtains, sneezing because of the dust in them. They were the winter curtains, nice warm velvet ones. Spells popped them all into the big basket.

Then he went out to do some shopping. "You mind the caravan while we shop," he told Bits, and off went Tumpy and Spells together.

Bits the dog was bored. He tried to find a comfortable place to lie in, but he couldn't. He wasn't allowed on the beds, and Tumpy had hung all the rugs out on a line outside, ready to beat them when he came back. Bits felt cross.

Then he saw the basket of velvet curtains. Ah! they looked comfortable and soft and warm. Tumpy and Spells wouldn't be back for some time. He could hop into the basket, snuggle between the curtains there and have a good sleep.

So Bits jumped in, snuggled on the velvet curtains, put his nose on his paws, and fell asleep. He was still asleep when Tumpy and Spells came back. They were in a hurry.

"What a bit of luck that we met the washerwoman!" said Tumpy. "Now she can take the curtains home with her and we can call for them on our way back in the caravan."

Mrs Suds was a big, strong woman. She could carry the basket on her shoulders easily. Tumpy shut down the lid, and fastened it. He gave it to Mrs Suds and watched her stagger off with it.

"I wouldn't have thought that curtains weighed so heavily," said Tumpy to Spells. "Well, let's go on our way, Spells. Hey, Caravan – put your best foot forward! Off we go again!"

The caravan set off. It hadn't gone very far before Tumpy realized Bits the dog was missing. "Where's Bits?" he said, looking in every corner of the caravan. "Hey, Bits! BITS! Where are you? Now, where's that dog gone?"

"Stop, Caravan, stop!" called Spells. "We've lost Bits." But the caravan didn't stop. It was enjoying a walk after its rest. It went a bit faster.

"Caravan! Do as you're told!" shouted Tumpy. "You are most disobedient today. Stop, I say!"

But the caravan began to run, and Tumpy sat down very suddenly. Things began to slide around inside the van.

"We'd better get out and try and find Bits," said Spells, anxiously. But Tumpy shook his head.

"No. With the caravan in this silly sort of mood we'll be left behind, Spells. Goodness knows where it will run to! We might lose it altogether. Oh, dear — where in the world can Bits be?"

Well, the caravan ran on all that day and all that night. "It's gone right past the washerwoman's village," said Spells, gloomily. "Now we shall lose our curtains, too. Really, this caravan wants a good telling off. Trotting on and on like this. What behaviour!"

Well, very fortunately, the caravan got a bit tired, so at the next village it came to, it stopped. Tumpy and Spells were very glad. They said a lot of furious things to the caravan, and then wondered what to do about looking for poor Bits. Where *could* he have got to?

"Hello! Who's this coming panting up to us?" said Tumpy, suddenly. "It looks like Mr Suds, the washerwoman's husband. And he's got our washing basket on his shoulder. Oh, good – Mrs Suds must have done the curtains."

It *was* Mr Suds. He set the basket down and gave Tumpy a bill. Tumpy stared in surprise.

"For washing three pairs velvet curtains, very dirty – three pounds.

"For washing one dog, also very dirty, fifty pence."

"Dog! – what dog?" said Tumpy, astonished. "We didn't send a dog to be washed."

"Yes, you did," said Mr Suds. "He was in the basket too. So Mrs Suds washed him and you won't know him, he's so clean. She's popped him into a paper bag, and he's in with the curtains."

Tumpy opened the lid of the basket – and out leapt poor Bits, looking so clean that Tumpy and Spells really didn't know him! He jumped up at them, and licked them till they were quite wet.

"Oh, Bits! You must have put yourself into the basket and got taken away to be washed!" said Tumpy, patting him. "How silly you are! Don't you do such a stupid thing again!"

"He won't," said Mr Suds. "He didn't like being washed at all. It's a good thing Mrs Suds didn't iron him like the curtains."

"Woof," said poor Bits, with his tail down. What a fuss Spells and Tumpy made of him that day! And will you believe it, the very first chance Bits had, he went and rolled himself in some mud. What a waste of fifty pence!

# The tale of Twisty and Ho-Ho

O nce upon a time Ho-Ho the Goblin went along by the fields to catch the bus that went to the market. He walked by the stream and sang as he walked, for it was a very pleasant day.

Ho-Ho was going to buy some cows for his master. He was to bring them home that evening. He had cut himself a big stick from the hedge, and with this he meant to drive the cows home. Ah, Ho-Ho felt very important today! He stood still for a moment and looked at the bubbling stream.

"The cows shall drink out of this stream," he said. "They will be thirsty, walking all the way home this hot day."

Now, as Ho-Ho stood watching the

sparkling water, he heard the sound of someone whistling, and he turned round to see who was coming. He saw Twisty the gnome coming along swinging a big stick as he went.

"Good morning, Twisty!" called Ho-Ho. "Where are you going?"

"I am going to the market to buy my master some sheep," said Twisty, "and this is the stick I have cut to drive them home!"

"Now that is a funny thing," cried Ho-Ho. "I am going to the market to buy my master some good cows that will be sold there today. And I have cut this stick to drive them home! We will catch the bus together, buy our animals together, and come home together!"

"Yes," said Twisty. "And my master said to me, 'Twisty,' he said, 'see that you give the sheep a drink on the way home, for they will be very thirsty walking so far on the dusty roads.' When I saw this stream I thought that this would be where they drank."

"No," said Ho-Ho at once. "They cannot drink here, Twisty."

"And why not?" asked Twisty.

"Because my cows will drink here tonight," said Ho-Ho. "And they will be very thirsty indeed, and will drink so much that there will be none left for your sheep."

"Then you must take your cows somewhere else to drink," said Twisty. "For certainly my sheep will drink here! I will not have your cows drinking from this stream, for, if they do, there will not be enough water for my sheep!"

"I tell you your sheep shall *not* drink here!" shouted Ho-Ho.

"And I tell you that your cows shall not drink here!" Twisty shouted back.

Ho-Ho banged his stick on the ground, and the dust flew up. "If you bring your sheep to this field, and let them drink from this stream, I shall drive them away," he said.

Twisty hammered his stick on the ground, and the dust flew up in such a cloud that Ho-Ho began to choke. "I tell you, Ho-Ho, if you bring your cows here tonight I shall push them all into the water!" shouted Twisty.

"Indeed you will not!" yelled Ho-Ho.

With that he struck out at Twisty with his stick. The gnome lifted his own stick and hit out at Ho-Ho. He knocked his hat off, and it fell into the water.

"There goes my best hat!" groaned Ho-Ho, and he stamped on the ground in rage. He poked Twisty hard with his stick, and the gnome over-balanced and fell splash into the stream!

He sat up in the water and shook his fist at Ho-Ho, who was standing on the bank laughing loudly. Out of the water jumped Twisty, shook himself like a dog, and jumped at Ho-Ho. Over and over on the grass they rolled, and at last down the bank of the stream they went together, *splish-splash* into the water. How they choked and spluttered as they lay in the water trying to get out!

"I've swallowed a fish!" said Twisty.

"I've swallowed two!" said Ho-Ho. "And see how wet I am!"

"So am I," said Twisty. "Let us get out and dry our clothes before we go to market. It will never do to go to market dripping wet."

So they climbed out of the stream and sat on the grass in the sun. They took off their coats and hung them on a tree nearby to dry.

And, as they sat there, drying, they heard on the road not far off the *rumble-rumble-rumble* of the bus. It was on its way to market, the only bus of the morning!

"The bus! The bus!" shouted Twisty, and he jumped to his feet. "Come, quickly, Ho-Ho, or we shall miss it."

They tore off over the field and came to the gate as the bus passed. It stopped when the driver saw them, and the two ran to it; but even as they took hold of the rail to pull themselves into the bus they remembered something.

Their coats! They had left them drying on the tree – and in the pockets of their coats was the money their masters had given them to buy the cows and the sheep! They could not go to market to buy without money.

"Wait a moment for us," begged Twisty. "We have left our coats in the field."

The gnome and the goblin raced over the field and took down their wet coats.

They turned to go back to the waiting bus, and Twisty said: "Well now, just you remember, Ho-Ho, on no account are you to bring your cows here tonight to drink from my sheep's stream!"

"What do you mean?" shouted Ho-Ho. "I told you I had chosen it for my cows, and that you were not to bring your sheep!"

Just as they stood glaring at one another they heard a *rumble-rumble-rumble* – and the bus had gone on down the lane! It would not wait any longer, for it was already late. It had gone, and

29

the two quarrellers were left behind.

They stared at the disappearing bus in dismay. It climbed the hill and went over the top. They could not get to market that morning.

"I shall have no cows to bring to the stream to drink," said Ho-Ho, in a small voice, "and my master will be very angry with me."

"And I shall have no sheep to bring to the stream to drink," said Twisty, "and my master will be so angry with me that I shall have no dinner and no supper."

"Why did we quarrel?" said Ho-Ho. "The stream is big enough to give water to all the sheep and cows in the market!"

"We were selfish!" cried Twisty. "We each wanted the whole stream for our animals, and now we have no animals to bring to the stream. It serves us right. Goodbye, Ho-Ho. I am going to tell my master that I have missed the bus."

"Goodbye," said Ho-Ho. "I must go back to the farm, too. Next time we meet, Twisty, we will be more sensible."

## *The flyaway balloon*

Auntie Mary gave a New Year's party to all her nieces and nephews. It was a very nice party with heaps of crackers, balloons and things to eat.

There was one balloon that had somehow got blown up much bigger than the others. It floated with them in a great big bunch, each balloon on its own string. It was very pleased with itself.

"How big I am!" it thought. "How very, very big! Much bigger than the others. I am a giant balloon, and if I had a long enough string I could fly up to that big balloon in the sky – what's it called, now? Oh, yes, the moon. I am sure I must be as big as the moon."

It wondered which child would have it. Auntie Mary wondered, too. It was such a lovely big blue balloon, with such a nice smiley face on it that she thought it really ought to be a prize for something.

"I'll give it as a prize for musical chairs," she thought. "Whoever wins musical chairs shall have that big balloon!"

Alice won it. She was very pleased. She took the great big balloon from her aunt and held it in her arms, squashing its firm softness against her.

"It feels lovely," she said. "It's a giant balloon. It will never, never burst!"

"Burst! Whatever does she mean?" thought the big balloon. "Why should I burst? I never, never will."

And then suddenly there was a loud POP near by. Somebody else's balloon had burst. All the children jumped, and so did the balloons. What a horrid noise! And where had that balloon gone? One minute it was a lovely big yellow thing – the next it had disappeared, and all that was to be seen was a tiny bit of dirty-looking rubber, torn and ragged, tied to the string.

The big balloon was alarmed. Was that what bursting meant? It didn't like the sound of it at all! Alice flung her big balloon into the air, holding it by its short string.

"Look – look! See how this enormous balloon flies!" she cried. "Isn't it a beauty! I'm sure it would fly like a kite if I had a long enough string and took it out in the wind."

The big balloon tried to reach the ceiling but it couldn't. The string held it back. Horrid string! The balloon wished it could get away from it.

Alice took the big balloon home. She hung it up in her bedroom at the end of the bed. The wind came in at the window and played with it, bobbing it about to and fro. It liked that.

The next day Alice took the big

balloon out in the wind on its string. Aha! The wind had a wonderful game with it, and blew it quite high in the air. But the string always pulled it back.

"I might be a dog on a lead, instead of a beautiful balloon that wants to fly up to the moon," thought the balloon, angrily. "Why doesn't Alice get me a longer string? Oh, I wish I could fly high!"

And then, next time the wind blew strongly, the balloon jerked so hard at the string that it slipped out of Alice's fingers – and the balloon at once shot high up into the air, far above the trees!

"I'm free, I'm free!" it thought, and its smiling face looked down on Alice. But the little girl was very upset. She began to cry. "You've gone! You were the biggest balloon I ever had – and now you've gone! You'll bump into something and burst. Oh, do, do be careful, balloon – don't bump into anything sharp!"

The balloon floated higher and

higher. It wanted to go to the clouds. Were they a kind of white balloon, too? And where was that moon? That should surely be hanging in the sky like a big silver balloon. Perhaps it would come when it was dark, and then the big balloon could fly up to it, and talk to it. It was sure it would be bigger than the moon!

The wind dropped. The balloon fell nearer to earth. Down, down, down. It came near to a tree. Be careful, balloon – that's a holly tree. BE CAREFUL! It is set with sharp prickles! You'll burst – you'll go POP!

A robin sang out sharply: "Go away! You'll go pop-bang! Go away!"

The balloon swerved away from the holly tree. Oh dear – what a narrow escape! What dreadfully sharp prickles it had nearly floated into.

It fell lower still. A sparrow chirruped loudly. "Balloon, be careful! That's barbed wire! It's set with sharp points. It will prick you and you'll BURST.

You'll go POP and we shan't see you any more!"

The balloon just missed the barbed wire. It was so alarmed that its smiling face didn't smile any more. It began to wish it was with Alice, on a nice short, safe string!

It fell to the ground and floated along, bumping up and down as it went. A rabbit saw it and ran after it, hitting it with its paw.

"Don't! You'll burst me!" cried the balloon in a squeaky, rubbery voice. The wind took it up into the air out of the rabbit's reach — but then down it fell again to the ground. This time it fell near a farm.

Two hens ran up. "What is it? Is it good to eat? Shall we peck it?"

"No, no, no! You'll burst me if you do!" cried the balloon. "Leave me alone!"

One of the hens gave the balloon a sharp peck. But it wasn't quite sharp enough and the balloon didn't burst, though it didn't like the peck at all. The

other hen ran at it – but the balloon just bobbed over a fence in time. Oh dear, what a life!

It bobbed into a field where a hungry goat stood. Aha! What was this, thought the goat, and trotted up to the balloon. Something to eat? Something big and round that would make a very nice meal?

The goat put his hoof on the balloon, just by the string round its neck. He bent his head down to eat it – but the wind gave a puff, and off went the balloon once more, shivering in fright. "Alice, Alice, where are you? Come and fetch me!" cried the poor balloon.

The goat hadn't burst it – but he had loosened the string at the bottom. Little by little the air began to escape out of the neck of the balloon. It grew smaller.

The wind took it along again, and, will you believe it, it blew the balloon right over the hedge into Alice's own garden! What a remarkable thing!

Alice was there and saw the balloon

at once. "Oh!" she cried, running to it. "What a tiny little balloon! I never saw such a teeny-weeny one in my life! You're a baby one!"

Well! The balloon was most astonished. It didn't know it had gone small and was getting even smaller.

But it suddenly saw that Alice's hands seemed very, very big – so it knew it was now very small. It wasn't a giant any more.

Alice took it indoors and put the balloon with her brother's and sister's balloons.

How tiny it was! The others laughed at it.

"Call yourself a balloon! You're a tiddler! Wherever did you come from?"

"I was once a giant balloon," said the balloon, humbly. "I thought I would fly up to the moon and see if I was as big as he is. But I've gone small."

"You're going smaller," said the pink balloon. "You'll soon be gone to nothing. Poor thing!"

He was right.

The balloon shrank until it was nothing but a tiny bit of blue rubber. It felt very small and humble and good-for-nothing.

"Oh! If only I were big as I was before, I wouldn't boast, or grumble at my string and want to fly to the moon!" thought the tiny bit of rubber. "I'd be sensible. But I've lost my chance. I'm no good to anyone now."

But next day Alice's father took the balloon, undid the string, and blew and blew and blew into it.

It swelled up – it got big and round and fat. It had a broad, smiling face. It was ENORMOUS!

"Why! It's the balloon I got at the party! It must be!" cried Alice. "I know its face – and it's just as big! Don't you slip your string again and fly away, balloon – you may never come back again. You may even BURST!"

"Don't worry. I'm sensible now," said the big balloon, bobbing on the string. "I don't want to fly to the moon. I just want to be kept on a string and be happy with what I've got."

Alice has still got it. She has blown it up five times altogether, but it's still there — and it's very, very old for a balloon, because she has had it for just over two years.

I've seen it — and I've flown it on its string.

And I do like its face. It smiles, and smiles, and smiles!

# *The Banana Man*

All the toys were very excited, because there was going to be a fancy dress party at midnight. There was to be a prize for the best dress of all, and another prize for the funniest.

"I'm going to dress up as the Fairy Queen," said the big doll.

"That's easy for you," said the baby doll. "You've only got to make yourself a crown and a pair of wings, because you have a dress fit for a queen already!"

"I'll make you a pair of fluffy ears and pin a tail on behind you and you can go as a rabbit, baby doll," said the teddy.

"Oh, thank you," said the doll. "That's kind of you. What will *you* go as, Teddy?"

"Something funny, I think," said the bear. "I can't win a prize for the best dress, but I might for the funniest."

"Tell me what you're going to be!" begged the pink cat. "I'll help you."

"Well, I don't know yet," said the bear. "So don't bother me. What are *you* going as, pink cat?"

"An elephant," said the pink cat.

"Don't be silly," said the baby doll. "You can't possibly go as an elephant."

"Well, I thought I could walk backwards and wave my tail so that everyone would think I was walking towards them waving my trunk," said the pink cat.

"You sound quite mad," said the bear. "You won't look like an elephant waving a trunk, you'll simply look like a rather silly cat walking backwards."

"Oh, don't quarrel," said the baby doll. "You go into a corner and think about what you're going to be, Teddy."

So the bear went and leaned against the waste-paper basket and tried to think of something. But he couldn't. Whatever could he dress up in? He really must choose something funny.

He smelt a sweetish smell. It came from the inside of the waste-paper basket. Teddy got up and looked inside. One of the children had eaten a banana and thrown the yellow skin there.

The teddy bear stared at it – and a great thought came into his head. Couldn't he get into that banana skin, ask the baby doll to sew the sides up for him, and make holes for his arms and legs – and his head would stick out of the top. He would be a Banana Man. Nobody had ever been a Banana Man before. It was a really wonderful idea!

He fetched the banana skin and went over to the baby doll. He told her about his idea and she giggled.

"Oh, dear! How everyone will laugh! It's the funniest dress I ever heard of. Now, let me make two holes at the bottom of the skin for your legs – there – I'll make the arm-holes later on when you're in the skin with your legs through their holes."

They went into a dark corner of the toy cupboard to finish the banana dress, and everyone wondered what the giggling in the corner was about.

But when it came to sewing up the skin, the baby doll couldn't do it. The cotton slipped in and out of the banana skin and the sides wouldn't hold together.

"It's no good," said the doll, in despair. "We'll have to get the elf in to do it for you. She's marvellous with her needle. I'll go and call her."

So she called the elf in, the one who had a cosy little home in the ivy outside the window. The elf took one look at Teddy in the banana skin and said, "Zips!"

"Pardon?" said the baby doll.

"Zips," said the elf. "That's what you need to keep these skins tightly done up. I'll go and get my zips, and put them in for you."

She ran off and soon came back with some zip-fastenings, which she put in the banana skins with a bit of magic. Then she zipped up the banana with the teddy bear inside!

The baby doll began to laugh. "Oh, dear – you do look so funny, Teddy! Your body is the banana, and your arms and legs and head are sticking out of it. You really look like a walking banana!"

The bear began to do a solemn dance, waving his arms and kicking up his legs. The elf and the baby doll laughed till they cried.

"You'll certainly win the prize for the funniest dress!" they said.

And he did. Nobody could help roaring with laughter at him. The pink cat was quite alarmed when he first saw him, because he had really no idea it was Teddy. He thought it was a live banana with arms and legs and a head!

The big doll got the prize for the most beautiful dress. The bear was very proud indeed when he had to go up and get the prize for the funniest. He capered all the way and the pink cat had to sit down because he was laughing so much that he kept falling over.

"So glad you got the prize, Teddy," said the elf. "I must run now, because I'm off to catch the night-bat to go and stay with my aunt. See you in two weeks' time. Goodbye!"

Off she went. Then the toys began to take off their fancy dresses and put them away. But dear me, the bear couldn't unzip his banana skin. It just wouldn't come undone.

The baby doll tried. The big doll tried, and the pink cat tried. But not one of them could unzip that banana.

"You know, the elf put the zips in with a touch of magic," said the big doll at last. "And *I* think it needs a touch of magic to get them undone again."

"The elf's gone away for two weeks," said the baby doll, remembering. "Oh, Teddy – you'll have to be a Banana Man for two whole weeks!"

"Whatever will the children say when they find me dressed up in a banana skin?" said the bear, in a small voice. "They won't know me. They won't like me, either. And certainly they won't take me to bed with them. Nobody would take a Banana Man to bed. Oh, dear – this is a very sad thing."

He was so upset about it that he sat down on his prize without knowing it; and as it was a lovely cream cake it didn't look much of a prize when the bear got up again.

"Lick it off me," said the bear, gloomily, to the pink cat. So the pink cat did, and really enjoyed it.

"Banana cream," said the pink cat. "Very nice indeed!"

Well, all this happened last week, and the bear is still a Banana Man, because the elf hasn't come back. And tomorrow the children mean to take him out to tea with them – so what they will say when they find him in the banana skin I really can't imagine. What would *you* say?

# A coat for the snowman

Old Mrs White looked out of her bedroom window and frowned. "Snow!" she said. "Snow – thick and white and deep! How annoying. What a lot must have fallen in the night."

"Oh, look at the lovely snow!" shouted the children in the field nearby. "It's as high as our knees. Let's build a snowman."

"Silly children to play with the cold snow like that," said Mrs White, who wasn't very fond of children. "Now I suppose they will play in the field all day and make a terrible noise. Bother them all."

Micky, Katie, Olive, Peter and Will played together in the snowy field that

day and had a lovely time. They made their snowman. He was a real beauty.

He had a big round head, with twigs sticking out for hair. He had eyes of stones and a big white stone for a nose. He had a stone for a mouth, too.

He had a big fat body, and the children patted it all round to make it smooth. He looked very real.

"We must dress him," said Micky. "We want a hat for him." He found an old hat in a ditch. It just fitted the snowman nicely. He wore it a little to one side and looked very knowing indeed.

"We want a scarf, too," said Katie. "My aunt lives in that cottage nearby. I'll see if she has one."

She had. It was an old red one, rather holey, but it went round the snowman's neck quite well.

"He'll feel warm with this scarf," said Olive. "It must be so cold to be made of snow. I do wish we had a coat for him to wear."

"Ooooh yes — then we could fill the sleeves with snow, and that would make him look awfully real," said Katie. "I'll ask my aunt for an old coat."

But her aunt said no, she hadn't a coat old enough for a snowman.

"Where can we get one?" asked Katie. "Shall I ask the old lady next door to you? What's her name? Mrs White?"

"Oh, you won't get anything out of *her*," said her aunt. "She doesn't like children. She's a grumbly old thing. You leave her alone."

"She looks very poor," said Olive. "Hasn't she got much money?"

"Hardly any," said Katie's aunt. "Don't you go bothering her, now — she'll box your ears if you do."

The children went back to their snowman. They looked at him. It would be so very, very nice if he had a coat. He would be the finest snowman in the world then.

Just then old Mrs White, in big rubber boots, came grumbling out to get herself a scuttleful of coal. Micky saw her.

"Poor old thing," he said. "I'll get the coal for her." He hopped over the fence and went down the snowy garden. Old Mrs White saw him and frowned.

"Now, what are you doing coming into my garden without asking?" she scolded.

"I'll get your coal in for you," said Micky. "Give me that shovel."

He shovelled until the scuttle was full. Then he carried it indoors for Mrs White.

"That's kind of you," she said. "But I hope you're not expecting money for that. I've none to spare."

"Oh no, of course not," said Micky, quite shocked. "My mother won't let me take money for doing bits of kindness. She says they're not kindnesses if you're paid for them. I don't want any reward at all, thank you, Mrs White."

"Well now, I wish I could give you something, that I do," said Mrs White, feeling pleased with the little boy. "But I've no biscuits and no sweets. You just look around my kitchen and tell me if there's anything you'd like now. What about that little china dog?"

"I don't want anything, thank you," said Micky, looking round. He suddenly saw an old, old coat hanging up behind the scullery door.

"Well," he said, "there's just one thing – do you think you could possibly lend us that old coat for our snowman, Mrs White? Only just *lend* it to us. We'll bring it back safely."

"Why, yes, if you want it," said old Mrs White. "It's a dirty, ragged old thing. I haven't worn it for years. I keep meaning to give it away. Yes, you take it. I shan't even want it back."

"Oh, thank you," said Micky. "Our snowman *will* look grand."

He unhooked the old coat from the door and ran back to the others with it. "Look what I've got!" he called. "Mrs White's given it to me for our snowman. Won't he look grand?"

The children filled the sleeves with snow and then hung the coat round the snowman. He certainly did look real now. There he stood in his old hat, scarf and coat, looking very fine.

"How do you do, Mr Shivers?" said Micky, walking up to the snowman and holding out his hand. "I hope you like this cold weather."

The others roared with laughter. The people passing by looked over the hedge at the snowman and called out that he was the best one they had seen. The children really felt very proud of him.

They left him standing there alone when it grew dark. But the next day they were back again. Alas, the snow had begun to melt, and Mr Shivers was a peculiar sight. He had slumped down, and all the snow had trickled out of his sleeves.

"He's going," said Micky. "I'll take my aunt's old scarf back to her."

"We don't need to take Mrs White's

coat back. She said we could keep it," said Peter. "Still, perhaps we'd better."

Micky jerked the coat off the melting snowman. He ripped the lining a little, and a piece of paper fell out.

"I say, what's this?" said Micky in surprise. "Why, it's paper money. It's a ten-pound note. It must have slipped out of the pocket into the lining, and old Mrs White didn't know it was there. Gracious, let's go and show it to her."

They all tore off to Mrs White's cottage. She could hardly believe her eyes when she saw the paper money. "Why, now, I lost that ten-pound note years and years ago," she said. "And proper upset I was about it, too. Thought I'd dropped it in the street, and all the time it was in my coat-lining. What a bit of good luck for me."

"Yes," said Katie. "I'm so glad."

"Bless your heart! What nice children you are. Maybe I've been wrong about boys and girls," said old Mrs White. "Well, well, now I can buy myself a new shawl and a new pair of shoes for my poor old feet."

She bought something else, too. She bought the biggest chocolate cake she could buy; she bought a pound of mixed biscuits, a pound of mixed chocolates, five big balloons and a big box of crackers. And she gave a party for Micky, Katie, Olive, Peter and Will.

They loved it. But in the middle of it Micky gave her quite a shock. "There's somebody who ought to have come to this party and isn't here," he said solemnly. "*What* a pity."

"Oh dear me, who's that?" said Mrs White, quite alarmed. "I *am* sorry I've forgotten one of you. Go and fetch him at once."

"We can't," said Micky, and he laughed. "It's Mr Shivers, the snowman, Mrs White. He ought to be the guest of honour, for without him we'd never have borrowed your coat and we wouldn't have found the money. What a pity old Mr Shivers isn't here."

# *Off with their shadows!*

"I hope those naughty little pixies don't come tonight," said the sailor doll. "They would spoil our nice party."

"They really are very mischievous," said the pink rabbit. "They upset the poor clockwork mouse very much by pretending they had thrown his key out of the window – and all the time it was in the brick-box."

"Yes – and they shouldn't have locked the dolls' house front door so that the little dolls couldn't get out," said the bear. "And they shouldn't have wound up the little car and set it running round the playroom all by itself, so that it knocked down half the Noah's Ark animals who were out walking!"

"Well, if they come tonight we will *not* let them join our party," said the sailor doll.

The party began. It was a bright moonlit night and the toys could see everything beautifully, because the moon looked in at the window all the time.

There was plenty to eat. The dolls' house dolls had been busy cooking all the evening on the little stove in their kitchen. The musical box played for dancing, and everything was very merry and bright.

And then those mischievous pixies arrived as usual! They flew in at the crack of the window and stood looking in delight at the party. "Hurrah! A party! Now we can join in and have a good time, too!"

"You can't come to a party if you're not invited," said the clockwork clown, and gave the nearest pixie a push.

"Oh, he pushed me, he pushed me!" cried the pixie. "Off with his shadow!"

The toys saw that the chief pixie had a little pair of scissors with her, and they were surprised.

"What do you mean – 'Off with his shadow'?" asked the curly-haired doll.

"Just what we say! Off with his shadow!" cried the pixies. "We're collecting shadows. We can sell them, you know. They make invisible cloaks. When anyone puts on a cloak made from shadows, he can't be seen! He becomes invisible at once."

"Good gracious! You don't *really* mean to say you're collecting shadows for that?" cried the pink rabbit. "How dare you?"

"Well, let us come to your party, then," said the pixies.

"No. We don't like you and we don't want you," said the teddy bear, quite fiercely. "You're just mischievous nuisances."

"Go away!" shouted the rest of the toys.

"Off with their shadows!" cried the

pixies in glee, and then, dear me, what a snip-snip-snipping there was!

The bear heard the scissors snipping behind him, and he turned in alarm. His nice fat little shadow was being snipped away where it stretched behind him. What a shame! The pixie rolled it up and threw it to another, who stuffed it into a bag.

Then the scissors went snipping behind the rabbit, and although he tried to run away, he couldn't until his shadow had been snipped from his feet and rolled up like the first one.

"Who's next, who's next?" cried the pixies. "Off with their shadows! They won't let us come to their party!"

Off went the curly-haired doll's big shadow and the clockwork mouse's tiny one. Off went the sailor doll's. What an upset there was, as the little black shadows were snipped away and thrown into the bag.

"Come into the dark corners!" cried the clockwork clown. "We don't have

shadows in the dark, dark corners.
Quick, join me over here!"

So all the rest of the toys ran to
the dark corners, where their shadows

couldn't be seen. The pixies laughed.

"We've got enough shadows to make a simply wonderful cloak to sell to Mr High-Hat the wizard," they shouted. "Goodbye! It serves you right for not letting us come to your party!"

Well, what a to-do there was when those mischievous pixies had flown out of the window! The toys who had had their shadows snipped off stood in the moonlight crying because they hadn't any shadows stretching out behind them.

"It isn't as if our shadows were ever much *good* to us," sobbed the little mouse. "But it's dreadful not to have them. I don't feel right without a shadow running about with me."

"I think we'd better go and complain to the old owl in the tree outside the window," said the pink rabbit. "He's very, very wise. Everyone knows that. He might know where the pixies have gone and go after them to get our shadows back for us."

So they called out through the crack in the window. "Hoo-hoo-hoo, the owl, are you there? We want your advice, please."

Hoo-hoo-hoo flew to the window-sill. The toys told him all about the mischievous pixies and how they had shouted "Off with their shadows!" and snipped them away to make a cloak.

"Ha! They tried to do that to me, too, when they thought I was sleeping on a bough – but I wasn't," said the owl. "They all fell off the branch in a hurry when I opened my eyes and hooted. Don't worry. I'll go after them and fetch your shadows back. Have a needle and black cotton ready to sew them on, because they will go out of shape if they are away from you for very long."

The toys got ready some needles threaded with black cotton, and waited anxiously for the owl to come back.

He came at last and sat on the window-sill. "Hoo-hoo, too-whit!" he said. "I'm back. But, toys, I'm sorry to say that those naughty little pixies have already sewn your shadows into a big cloak."

"Oh, dear!" said the toys in dismay. "What are we to do, then?"

The owl began to laugh. "Ho-ho-ho, hoo-hoo-hoo! I told those pixies I would pick them up in my big talons and drop them in the very middle of the pond if they didn't give me some shadows to take back to you!" he said.

"And did they?" cried the toys.

"Yes! They were so scared that they cut each other's shadows off, rolled them up and gave them to me," said the owl, and he showed them something he was holding in his left foot. "Here they are, all ready for you."

"Oh, thank you, thank you, thank you!" said the toys, in delight, and they caught the little soft bundle of shadows that the owl pushed through the window crack.

"Quick — we must sew them on before

they lose their shape," said the sailor doll – and you should have seen how busy they all were, sewing on those shadows to the heels of the toys that had lost them.

At last they were all on. "Oh, good!" said the clockwork mouse. "It's nice to have a shadow again. Let's go and stand in the bright moonlight and see if they are exactly like our own shadows."

So they went to stand in the moonlight – and the rabbit gave a shout. "I say! Look at *my* shadow! It's got wings!"

"So has *my* shadow – and pointed ears like pixies have!" cried the teddy bear. "*I* haven't got ears like that. Oh, dear – my shadow does look strange!"

"It's the shadow of a *pixie*," said the curly-haired doll. "Mine's like that, too. Look – it's got pointed ears, a little head – and wings! It's nice to have a shadow with wings. I've always wanted wings, and I shall feel as if I've got them when I look at my winged shadow!"

Wasn't it strange — each toy that had lost his own shadow had a pixie shadow now! What could they do about it? Nothing at all! Their own shadows were made up into a magic cloak and given to the wizard. They had to put up with pixie shadows instead.

They really felt rather grand, and the toys whose shadows hadn't been cut off felt quite jealous. They would have liked pixies' shadows, too!

But *what* do you suppose the children will say when they next play with their toys? They will stand up the sailor doll — and see that his shadow belongs to a pixie! The rabbit will show a pixie shadow, too, and so will the little clockwork mouse! What a thrill for the children! They won't know what to make of it, will they?

I do hope they will read this story, and then they will know exactly what has happened. If they do, I shall expect them to write to me and ask me to come and see the toys with the pixie shadows.

# The little brownie house

**K**im and Mickle were very worried. They were brownies who lived in a tree house like Josie, Click, and Bun – and now the woodman had come to chop down their tree.

"We shall have to move," said Kim. "And quickly too, or the tree will come down and all our furniture with it! Hurry, Mickle, and get it all out."

So the brownies took their furniture on their shoulders and piled it on the grass outside. There it stood, and there the brownies stood too, wondering where to go.

They borrowed a hand cart from Bonny the pixie and put the furniture on it, ready to wheel away. But there really seemed nowhere at all to go. There had been so many old trees cut down in the wood that many people had taken all the empty houses there were.

"There's not even a hole in a grassy bank we can have," said Kim. "At least, there's one – but the fox lives there, and he doesn't smell very nice."

"Oh, we can't go there," said Mickle. "We'd have to hold our noses!"

"Well, let's wheel our barrow round a bit and see if there's any empty house we can go to," said Kim. So, with the noise of the woodman's axe ringing in their ears, they wheeled their cart away, with their two little beds, their two little chairs, their table, cupboard, curtains and mats on it, looking rather sad.

They came at last to a high hedge. At the bottom was a gap, so they wheeled the barrow through – and there in a garden was a little empty house! It was painted brown, and had a big open doorway.

"I say! Look at this!" cried Kim, running to it. "An empty house – just our size too! What about living here? There's nothing in the house at all, except some old straw."

"It's fine," said Mickle. "But it's rather a funny house, Kim – there's no door – and no window either!"

"Well, that doesn't matter, Mickle!" said Kim. "We can easily make a door, and just as easily make a window! Oh, Mickle – it will be fun living in this little house, won't it!"

Well, the two brownies moved in. The house was exactly right for them. They put in their beds, one on each side of the room, for the house had only the one room. "Our beds can do for sofas, in the daytime," said Kim.

They put the table in the middle, and the chairs beside it. They put the cupboard at the back, and spread the rugs on the floor. You can't think how lovely it all looked when it was done.

They had a tiny jam jar and Kim went

to fetch some daisies for it. He put the vase of daisies in the middle of the table.

Mickle put the clock on the cupboard and wound it up. Tick-tick-tock-tock! it went.

"There now," said Kim. "Flowers on the table — and a clock ticking. It's home, real home, isn't it?"

The brownies were very happy. The little house looked out on to a garden belonging to a big house built of brick. People lived there, and two children often came out of the house to play. But they never came to the brownies' house.

"It's a good thing our house is right at the bottom of the garden, where nobody ever comes," said Kim. "Now, Mickle — what about making a door? The rain came in yesterday and wet the carpet."

So the two brownies set about making a door. They found a nice piece of wood, and with their tools they made it just the right size for a door. They painted it blue, and hung it in the doorway with two little brass hinges. It opened and shut beautifully.

They put a knocker on it and made a slit for a letterbox. It did look nice.

"And now we'd better make two little windows," said Mickle. "When we have the door shut our house is very dark and stuffy. We will make a little window each side and find some glass to put in."

So they carved out two squares for windows, and found an old glass bottle by the garden frames. They cut two pieces of glass out of the bottle to the right size, and fitted them in. Then they cleaned the windows, and hung up blue curtains.

"Really, it looks simply lovely now!" said Kim. "The door is such a nice blue and the knocker shines so brightly, and the curtains at the window look so pretty. I think we ought to have a party."

"Yes, we ought," said Mickle. "But if we give a party, we must make cakes. And we can't bake cakes unless we have an oven and a chimney – and there isn't a chimney, you know."

So they made a chimney, and bought a nice little oven from the pixie down the way. They fixed it into the corner, and then lit a fire. The smoke went straight up the chimney and away into the garden. It was marvellous! The oven cooked beautifully, and what a delicious smell came from it the first time that the brownies cooked buns and cakes!

They sent out the invitations to the party. "Everyone will love our little house," said Kim. "They will think we are very, very lucky to have found it. I do wonder who it belonged to. We have never heard."

Now, on the day of the party, Kim and Mickle began to do a great cleaning and cooking. All the mats were shaken, the windows were cleaned, the knocker was polished, and the stove cooked cakes, buns, and biscuits without stopping. It was great fun.

And then something extraordinary

happened! A voice outside the house cried out, "Look at this! There's somebody living here!"

The brownies peeped out of the window and saw two children, a boy and girl, staring in the greatest astonishment at their house. "Goodness!" said Mickle. "Do you suppose it's *their* house, and they want to come back and live in it? Oh dear, I do hope they won't turn us out!"

"We'd better go and ask them," said Kim. But before he could do that, somebody knocked at the door. They used the little knocker – rat-a-tat-tat! Kim opened the door. He saw the two children looking down at him in delight and surprise.

"Hallo!" said the boy. "Do you really live here?"

"Yes," said Kim. "I hope you don't mind. It was empty when we found it, and there was nobody to say who it belonged to. Do *you* want to come and live here?"

The children laughed and laughed. "No, you funny little thing!" said the girl. "Of course we don't. We live in that big house up the garden."

"Oh, this isn't your house?" said Kim.

"It used to be our dog's kennel," said the boy with a giggle. "But we don't keep a dog now, so the kennel has been empty for a long time. Today we saw smoke at the bottom of the garden, and we came down to see what it was. And we suddenly saw a chimney on our dog's kennel, and two little windows, and a front door with a knocker!"

"We *did* get a surprise!" said the girl. "But oh, it's simply lovely! You have made the kennel into the prettiest little house I ever saw in my life!"

"So it was your dog's kennel!" said Mickle. "Oh, I do hope you won't want it for another dog."

"No, Mummy says dogs bark too much," said the boy. "So you're quite safe."

"May we really go on living here, then?" asked Kim, in delight.

"Of course," said the girl. "We'll never tell anyone about you, we promise. But please, please may we sometimes come down, knock at your door, and talk to you? You know, it's very exciting to have a brownie house at the bottom of our garden, with real brownies living there."

"You *are* nice," said Mickle. "Listen – we're having a party this afternoon. Would you like to come? You can't get inside the house comfortably, I'm afraid, but you could eat buns and biscuits out on the grass."

The two children squealed for joy. "Oh, *yes!*" said the girl. "Do, do let us come. We shall see all your friends then. And oh, little brownie, would you like me to lend you my best dolls' tea set for the party? It's very pretty, with a blue and yellow pattern."

"Thank you very much," said Mickle. "We haven't really got enough cups and plates, and we'd love to borrow yours."

So they borrowed the tea set, and it looked lovely in the little brownie house, set out on the round table. The party was simply lovely – but the two who enjoyed it most were the children, as you can guess. It was such a treat to sit and look at all the little folk coming to the dog's kennel, dressed in their best, knocking at the blue door, and saying "How do you do" to Mickle and Kim!

I won't tell you the names of the children, in case you know them – because they don't want anyone else to visit the brownie house and frighten away their tiny friends. But don't you think they're lucky to have a dog kennel that is used by Mickle and Kim?

# *You bad little dog*

John and Freda took their little dog
Wuff down to the sands with them.
It was such a lovely beach for little dogs,
as well as for children!

There was fine golden sand stretching
right down to the very edge of the sea
– and tiny waves to play in, and warm
pools to bathe in. Wuff liked it as much
as John and Freda did.

That morning the children had their
spades with them. They meant to build
the biggest castle on the beach – bigger
even than Tom and Peter and Dick had
built the week before. That one was so
big that the sea just couldn't knock it
all down, but left half of it for the next
day.

Wuff wanted to build, too – but as his idea of building was to dig enormous holes and scatter the sand all over the place, John and Freda wouldn't let him help.

"No," they said. "You keep away today, Wuff. You're just being a nuisance. As soon as we get a heap built up you scrape a hole in it. That's not building!"

So Wuff went a little way away and sat down sadly to look at the two children building. Soon an old man came and sat down in a deckchair nearby. He opened his newspaper and began to read. He wasn't near the children, and they took no notice of him at all.

But Wuff was quite near him, sitting still, feeling rather bored. He suddenly smelt rather a nice smell. He got up and ambled round and about, sniffing at the sand. Ah – here was the smell!

Someone had left a bit of cake in the sand and Wuff felt that he really must dig it up. So he began to scrape violently with his front paws. Up into the air went great showers of fine sand – and the old man found himself being covered from head to foot.

"Stop it," he growled to Wuff. But Wuff was too happy to hear. He was getting near that bit of cake! Up flew some more sand, and down it came on the old man's newspaper, making a little rattling noise.

The man jumped up in anger. He picked up some seaweed and threw it at Wuff. "Bad dog, you! Go away! They shouldn't allow dogs on the beach. I've always said so! Grrrrr!"

The seaweed hit Wuff and he yelped and ran off. He was frightened, too, when the man made the growling noise because it sounded like a big dog!

The children were very cross when they saw the old man throwing seaweed at Wuff and heard him shouting. "Just because Wuff threw some sand over him by mistake!" said Freda.

"You take that nasty little dog of yours away from this beach!" shouted the old man. "If he comes near me again he'll be sorry!"

Freda and John were upset. They left their castle half-finished, and Wuff left the hidden bit of cake, and they all went right to the other end of the beach. They began to build another castle, but it was dinner-time before they had done very much. They were very disappointed.

"Now the sea will be able to sweep away all we've done," said John. "The castle ought to be twice as high if there's to be any left when the tide goes out again."

They went home to dinner, Wuff dancing round their legs. The old man had gone, too. The deckchair was empty and the chair-man was just about to pile it with all the others, so that the sea wouldn't take it away when the tide came in.

Next morning the children went down to the beach again. Wuff went, too. The old man was there in his chair, and John and Freda decided not to go too near him.

"We really must work hard this morning," said John. "Granny is coming this afternoon and it would be lovely to show her a really magnificent castle, bigger than any on the beach."

"Wuff," said Wuff, quite agreeing.

"You go away till we've finished," said Freda to Wuff. "Look, take your ball and go over there to play with it. You aren't much good at castles, Wuff."

Wuff took his ball. But it was really very boring to play by himself, and he suddenly remembered the bit of cake he had smelt in the sand the day before. Suppose it was still there? He could perhaps find it this time. He began to run about, sniffing, to see if he could smell it again.

He came near to the old man and stopped. Why, here was the man who growled like a dog and threw seaweed at him! He'd better be careful or he might be hit by another piece of soggy seaweed.

The old man sat quite still. He didn't speak or move. Wuff sniffed the air. Was he asleep? When people were asleep they didn't shout or throw things. He could look for that bit of cake if the old man was asleep.

He *was* asleep – fast asleep in the warm sun. His newspaper lay on his knee. The wind tugged at it, trying to get it.

Wuff began to scrape in the sand for the bit of cake. A few grains flew into the air and fell on the newspaper on the man's knee. He didn't stir at all. The wind suddenly blew strongly and the newspaper flapped hard. It flapped itself right off the man's knee on to the sand.

Wuff stopped burrowing and looked at it. Soon that newspaper would blow right away. He didn't know why people liked newspapers so much, but he knew they did. This one belonged to the old man. Did he want it? Would he mind if his paper blew right into the sea?

The children suddenly saw Wuff near the old man again. They called to him. "Wuff! Wuff! Come away from there! You know you got into trouble yesterday."

Then John saw the newspaper blowing away. "Look," he said, "the paper has blown off that man's knee. He must be asleep. There it goes! Oh, won't he be cross when he wakes up and finds that the sea has got it!"

"It will serve him right for throwing seaweed at Wuff," said Freda.

"There goes the paper – almost into that pool," said John. "Wuff – fetch it, then, fetch it, boy!"

Wuff raced after the paper and pounced on it just before it flew into the pool! The old man, awakened by the shouting, sat up and looked round to see what the noise was about.

He saw Wuff pouncing on his paper – and then the little black dog turned and ran all the way back to the old man with it and put it down by his feet, just as he did when he ran after a ball and took it back to the children.

"Why, you good, clever dog!" said the old man, patting him. "Fine dog, good dog! Who do you belong to?"

"He belongs to us," said John and Freda, coming up, astonished to find the man making such a fuss of Wuff.

"Well, he's a very clever dog," said the man, folding up his newspaper. "Not a bit like a horrid little dog I saw here yesterday, who threw sand all over me. Oh, he was a dreadful little thing!"

"Wuff!" said Wuff, trying to tell the man that yesterday's dog and today's were exactly the same. But the man didn't understand.

"I must buy a bone for this good dog," said the man. "Does he like bones?"

"Yes. But he likes ice-creams even better," said Freda.

"Well, well – what good taste he has!"

said the man, getting up. "Shall we all go and buy ice-creams? Come along, then."

They went to the ice-cream man and the old man bought four ice-creams, one for each of them and one for Wuff too, of course. Then he went down to look at the castle the children were building.

"I'd better help you with this," he said. "I can see you won't finish it if I don't. We'll make it the biggest one ever seen!"

They finished their ice-creams, Wuff too, and set to work. My goodness me, how the old man could dig! You should have seen that castle when it was finished. All the children on the beach came to admire it.

"Well, thank you very much indeed for the ice-creams and the digging," said John and Freda.

"I'll help you again tomorrow," said the man, smiling. "Goodbye – and goodbye, little dog. I'm glad you're not like the nasty little dog I shouted at yesterday!"

Off he went. The two children looked at one another. "Well! He may think Wuff is a different dog – but honestly *he's* a different man, too!" said John. "Who would have guessed he could be so nice?"

It *was* funny, wasn't it? What a good thing Wuff ran after his paper!

## The cat without whiskers

Inky was a black cat, with the finest white whiskers in the street. He was a handsome cat, with sharp ears and a long thick tail that looked like a snake when he waved it to and fro. He had a white mark under his chin which the children called his feeder, and he washed it three times a day, so that it was always like snow.

Inky was plump, for he was the best ratter and mouser in the town, and never lacked a good dinner. When he sat on the wall washing himself he was a fine sight, for his glossy fur gleamed in the sun and his whiskers stuck out each side of his face like white wires.

"I'm the finest-looking cat in the

town," said Inky proudly, and he looked scornfully down at the tabby in the garden below, and the white cat washing itself on a window-sill near by. "Nobody is as good-looking as me!"

Then there came by a little boy, and when he saw the big black cat sitting up on the wall, he shouted up at him, laughing, "Hallo, Whiskers!"

Inky was offended. His name wasn't Whiskers. It was Inky. A little girl heard what the boy said and she laughed. "That's a good name for him," she said. "He's a very whiskery cat. Whiskers! Whiskers!"

Everyone thought it a funny name, and soon Inky was being called Whiskers all day long, even by the cats and dogs around. This made him really very angry.

"It's a horrid, silly name," he thought crossly, "and it's rude of people to call me that. They don't call that nice old gentleman with the beard 'Whiskers',

do they? And they don't shout 'Nosy' at that boy with the big nose. I shan't answer them when they call me Whiskers!"

So he didn't – but it wasn't any good, for everyone shouted "Whiskers! Whiskers!" as soon as they saw Inky's wonderful whiskers.

Inky thought hard. "I shall get rid of my whiskers," he said to himself. "Yes

– I shall start a new fashion for cats. We won't have whiskers. After all, men shave every morning, and people think that is a good idea. I will shave my whiskers off, and then no one will call me Whiskers."

He told his idea to wise old Shellyback the tortoise. Shellyback listened and pulled at the grass he was eating.

"It is best not to meddle with things you have been given," he said. "You will be sorry."

"No, I shan't," said Inky. "My whiskers are no use to me that I can see – I shall shave them off!"

Well, he slipped into the bathroom at his home early the next morning and found the thing his master called a razor. In a trice Inky had shaved his beautiful whiskers off. They were gone. He was no longer a whiskery cat.

He looked at himself in the glass. He did look a bit strange – but at any rate no one would now shout Whiskers after him. He slipped down the stairs and out into the garden. He jumped on the wall in the sun.

The milkman came by and looked at him. He did not shout "Whiskers!" as he usually did. He stared in rather a puzzled way and said nothing at all. Then a little boy came by delivering papers, and he didn't shout "Whiskers!" either.

Inky was pleased. At last he had got rid of his horrid name. He sat in the sun, purring, and soon his friends gathered round him. There was Tabby from next door, the white cat Snowball, Shellyback the tortoise, who looked up at him from the lawn, and the old dog Rover, who never chased cats.

"What's the matter with you this morning, Inky?" asked Snowball, puzzled. "You look different."

"His whiskers are gone," said Tabby, startled. "How strange."

"How did you lose them?" asked Rover.

"I shaved them off," said Inky

proudly. "I am starting a new fashion for cats. Grown-up men shave their whiskers off each day, don't they? Well, why should cats have whiskers? Don't you think I look much smarter now?"

Everyone stared at Inky, but nobody said a word. They all thought Inky looked dreadful without his whiskers.

"You'll soon see every animal following my fashion of no whiskers," said Inky. "It's so much more comfortable. Whiskers always get in my way when I'm washing my face, but now I can wash it as smoothly as anything. Look!"

He washed his face with his paw. Certainly it looked easier to do it without whiskers. But the older animals shook their heads.

"Whiskers are some use or we wouldn't have them," said Tabby.

"Well, what use *are* they?" said Inky.

But nobody was clever enough to think of anything to say in answer to that. One by one they slipped off to their homes to dinner, quite determined that *they* were not going to shave off their whiskers, whatever Inky did.

Now that night Inky felt very hungry. He had been late for tea that afternoon and a stray dog had gone into his garden and eaten up the plate of fish and milk that his mistress had put out for him. Inky was annoyed.

"Never mind," he thought to himself. "I'll go hunting tonight. I'll catch a few mice and perhaps a rat or two. I know a good place in the hedge at the bottom of the garden. I'll hide on one side of it and wait for the night animals to come out."

So off he went when darkness came and crouched down on one side of the hedge. Soon he heard the pitter-pattering of little mice-feet. Inky stiffened and kept quite still. In a moment he would squeeze through the hedge and pounce on those foolish mice.

He took a step forward. His paw was like velvet and made no noise. He pushed his head into a hole in the hedge – then his body – but alas for Inky! His body was too big for the hole, and the hedge creaked as he tried to get through. The mice heard the noise and shot off into their holes. Not one was left.

"Bother!" said Inky crossly. "I'll wait again. I believe that old rat has a run here somewhere. I'd like to catch him!"

So he waited – and sure enough the big rat ran silently by the hedge. Inky heard him and began to creep towards him; but his fat body brushed against some leaves and the rat heard and fled.

Inky was astonished. Usually he could hunt marvellously without making a single sound. Why was it that his body seemed so clumsy tonight? Why did he brush against things and make rustling noises? It was most annoying.

And then suddenly he knew the reason why. Although he hadn't thought about it, his fine whiskers had always helped him to hunt. They had stretched out each side of his face, and were just about the width of his body. He had known that if he could get his head and whiskers through a hole without touching anything, his body would go through easily too, without a sound.

"It was my whiskers that helped my

body to know if it could go easily and silently through the holes and between leaves," thought Inky in despair. "Of course! Why didn't I think of that before? They were just the right width for my body, and I knew quite well if I touched anything with my whiskers that my body would also touch it and make a noise – and so I would go another way!"

Inky was quite right. His whiskers had helped him in his hunting. Now he would not be able to hunt well, for he would never know if his body could squeeze through gaps and holes. He would always be making rustling, crackling noises with leaves and twigs. He would never catch anything. Poor Inky!

You can guess that Inky was always waiting for his mistress to put out his dinner after that – for he hardly ever caught a mouse or rat now. He grew much thinner, and he hid himself away, for he was ashamed to think that he had shaved off the things that had been so useful to him.

"A new fashion indeed!" thought Inky. "I was mad! If only I had my lovely whiskers again I wouldn't mind being called "Whiskers" a hundred times a day. My life is spoilt. I shall never be able to hunt again."

He was a sad and unhappy cat, ashamed to talk to anyone except wise old Shellyback the tortoise. One day he told Shellyback why he was unhappy. Shellyback looked at him closely and laughed.

"Go and sit up on the wall in the sun and see what happens," he said to Inky. "You'll find your troubles are not so big as you thought they were."

In surprise Inky jumped up on the wall and sat there in the sun. The milkman came by with his cart. He looked up.

"Hallo, Whiskers!" he shouted. "Good old Whiskers!"

Inky nearly fell off the wall in astonishment. What! He was called Whiskers again even if he had shaved them off? But silly old Inky had quite forgotten something. What had he forgotten?

He had forgotten that whiskers grow again like hair. His whiskers had grown out fine and long and strong and white – and he had been so miserable that he hadn't even noticed. Silly old Whiskers!

He *was* happy when he found that he had them again. He sat and purred so loudly that Shellyback really thought there was an aeroplane flying somewhere near! It sounded just like it.

And now Inky can hunt again, and is the best mouser in the town. He has grown plump and handsome, and his whiskers are finer than ever. He loves to hear himself called "Whiskers" now. So if you see him up on the wall, black and shining, don't say "Hallo, Inky!" – shout "Good old Whiskers!" and he'll purr like a kettle on the boil!

# Amelia Jane and the sailor doll

Once a new sailor doll came to the playroom where Amelia Jane and the rest of the toys lived. He was such a chatterbox.

"You know, sailors have adventures, plenty of them," he said. "And you should just hear mine . . ."

"We don't want to," said Amelia Jane. "You've told us about twenty times already."

"You're the rudest doll I've ever met," said the sailor doll huffily. "Well, as I was saying, one day when I was out at sea in my ship – I was the captain, of course – an enormous storm blew up, and the ship rocked to and fro, to and fro, just like a . . ."

"Rocking-horse," said Amelia with a giggle.

"Please be quiet," said the sailor. "Well, I somehow steered the ship to land and everyone was saved. Another time I went out in a lifeboat to rescue two people who couldn't swim. I got a medal for that. Look."

"It's not a medal," said Amelia Jane. "It's a button you picked up at the back of the toy cupboard. It's been there for ages."

"I don't believe you've ever *been* in a ship or a boat," said the clockwork mouse. "You just talk and talk."

Well, the sailor doll wasn't going to stand any rudeness from the mouse, and he chased him all round the room. Then he made a face at Amelia Jane and turned his back on her. He began talking all over again.

"*How* can we stop him from going on and on about adventures I'm sure he never had?" said the teddy bear. "He just goes on and on."

Well, Sailor went on like that till a day came when the children took the toys out into the garden for a picnic. They took little chairs and tables, too, for the toys to sit on, and gave them tiny cups of lemonade and plates full of biscuit crumbs. The toys really enjoyed themselves.

After the picnic, the children went indoors and left the toys by themselves. They were beside the little round pond where water-lilies floated on the water. Amelia Jane wanted to take off her shoes and paddle in the water. She called to the sailor doll.

"Come on, Sailor! You love the water, don't you? Let's paddle up to our knees, and you could take off your suit and have a swim, if you wanted to."

"I don't want to," said Sailor.

"You could sit on a water-lily leaf and have a very nice time," said Teddy.

"Don't be silly," said Sailor.

"Well, just come and wet your toes," said the pink rabbit. "Come on, you're always talking about what a wonderful life it is on the water. Here's plenty for you!"

"I'm sleepy," said the sailor doll. "Leave me alone. I wish there was somewhere soft and cosy to curl up — I'd have a nap in the sun."

Amelia Jane stared at him and a wicked look came into her eyes. "I know what you can do!" she said. "Look!"

She took hold of a toy table and turned it upside-down. She took some small cushions off the toy chairs and tucked them into the upside-down table. It looked a bit strange with its four legs sticking up into the air.

"A nice cosy bed for you!" said Amelia to Sailor. "Get in and have a nap. You *do* look tired."

Sailor was surprised to have so much kindness from Amelia Jane. He got into the table-bed and lay down. He yawned

loudly. "Nobody is to disturb me," he said.

"No, Your Majesty," said the clockwork mouse with a giggle.

Sailor frowned and closed his eyes.

"Don't disturb him," whispered Amelia Jane to the others. "Let him go fast asleep."

They were all puzzled. Why was Amelia being so nice to the sailor doll? Nobody liked him much. "I'll tell you in a minute," she whispered.

Soon the sailor doll began to snore. He often snored, and usually Amelia Jane tried to stop him. But she didn't this time. She tiptoed to the table-bed and smiled all over her face. She beckoned to Teddy, the clockwork mouse and the pink rabbit.

"We'll carry the upside-down table to the pond," she whispered. "And we'll set it floating on the water like a little boat. Whatever will he say when he wakes up?"

The clockwork mouse giggled so loudly that the bear gave him a sharp push. "Be quiet! You'll wake Sailor!"

Very gently the four toys each took one leg of the table and carried it to the pond. They set it down on the water, and Amelia gave it a push. It floated off beautifully to the middle of the pond, bumping into a yellow water-lily as it went. The goldfish were very surprised. They popped their red noses out of the water and had a good look.

"There he goes," said Amelia Jane with a chuckle. "He's got a boat at last! Hello, Captain! Hey, Captain, wake up, you're on a voyage to far away lands!"

The sailor doll woke up with a jump. He frowned. Hadn't he told the toys he wasn't to be disturbed? He turned over crossly on his cushions, and put one hand out over the edge of the floating table.

He got a sudden shock. Goodness! He had put his hand into something cold and wet! He sat up in a hurry.

He gazed round in fright. He was bobbing on the pond! Goodness gracious, what had happened! Why, the land seemed a long, long way away! He saw the toys standing on the edge of the pond, laughing.

"How did I get here?" he shouted. "Save me, quick!"

"You're the captain of your boat!" shouted Amelia. "You're sailing far away. You're having an adventure! Ooooh – mind a storm doesn't blow up!"

"I don't like it!" wailed Sailor, clinging to one of the table-legs. "I feel sick."

"He's sea-sick," said the clockwork mouse.

"No, pond-sick," said Teddy with a grin. "Our brave and wonderful Sailor, who has been through so many marvellous adventures, feels sea-sick on the pond. Hello – here comes the rain!"

*Plop, plop, plop!* Great raindrops fell on Sailor. The wind blew a little and ripples came on the pond. The table-boat bobbed up and down, and sailed all by itself into the very middle of the water-lilies.

"Help! Help!" yelled Sailor. "I shall drown! I shall fall in and drown!"

"Swim then!" shouted the rabbit, enjoying himself. "Swim like you say

you do when you go and rescue people."

"I can't swim!" wailed Sailor. "I can't, I can't! Save me!"

"The table's bobbing about on those little waves – I think it will turn over," said the clockwork mouse. "Sailor! Your boat may sink! Get out and sit on one of those water-lily leaves – they are so nice and flat!"

Sailor really was afraid that his table-boat would sink. He jumped on to a big, flat water-lily leaf. He sat down on it – and immediately it sank beneath him, and there he was, sitting in the water, yelling at the top of his voice.

"Goodness! He'll drown! He really and truly *can't* swim, for all the tales he's told us!" said the bear suddenly. "Look, he's slipping off that leaf – he's right in the water! I must save him!"

And, will you believe it, the fat old teddy bear suddenly plunged into the pond and began to swim as fast as he could towards poor old Sailor! Wasn't it brave of him?

Sailor clutched hold of him and Teddy swam back, puffing and panting. All the toys crowded round. They patted Teddy on his dripping wet back, and told him he was very, very brave.

"*I've* had an adventure now!" said Teddy, trying to squeeze water out of his furry little ears. "I swam out and saved somebody."

"Yes. But *your* adventure is a true one and Sailor's never are," said Amelia Jane. "Are they, Sailor?"

Sailor was standing all alone, his clothes making a puddle of wetness round his feet. He looked very much ashamed of himself. "Thank you, Teddy," he said in a small voice. "You were very brave – braver than I've ever been."

"That's the way to talk!" said the pink rabbit, pleased. "Come on – the sun's out again, so you and Teddy can sit in this sunny corner and get dry. Whatever will the children say if they find you dripping wet?"

Well, both Teddy and Sailor were dry when the children came back – but the little table still floated upside down on the pond! How surprised they were to see it there.

"Cushions in it, too!" they said. "What *have* the toys been up to?"

The toys didn't say a word, of course, but Amelia Jane looked even naughtier than usual.

And now, when Sailor forgets himself and begins one of his tales, Teddy interrupts at once, in a very loud voice, and begins his own tale.

"Once I swam out to rescue a silly sailor doll who couldn't even *swim*. It was a wonderful adventure for me. I'll tell you all about it."

And then, of course, Sailor stops boasting at once and creeps away. A sailor doll who couldn't swim! He will never, never be allowed to forget that.

What naughty things you do, Amelia Jane! However do you think of them?

114

# *Amelia Jane again!*

D o you remember Amelia Jane, the doll who didn't know how to behave herself because she was homemade, and didn't come from a shop?

Well, for a long time she was very good – and then, oh dear, she forgot all her promises and became really naughty! The things she did!

She took a needle and cotton out of the workbasket and sewed up the sleeves of the teddy bear's new coat when he wasn't looking. So when he went to put on his coat, he simply could *not* put his arms through the sleeves at all! They just couldn't find the way in – because the sleeves were sewn up! How Amelia Jane laughed to see him!

The next night she hid behind the curtain and began to mew like a cat. The toys were not very fond of Tibs the cat, because he sometimes chewed them. So they all stopped playing and looked round to see where Tibs was.

"I can hear him mewing!" said the teddy bear. "He must be behind the door."

But he wasn't. Amelia mewed again. The toys hunted all about for the cat. They even looked under the rug, which made Amelia laugh till she nearly choked! She mewed again, very loudly.

"Where *is* that cat?" cried the pink rabbit in despair. "We've looked everywhere! Is he behind the curtain?"

"No, there's only Amelia Jane there!" said the curly-haired doll, looking. "There's no cat."

Well, of course, they didn't find any cat at all! And Amelia Jane didn't tell them it was she who had been mewing, so to this day they wonder where Tibs hid herself that night!

Then Amelia Jane saw a soda water syphon left in a corner of the room. She knew how they worked, because she had seen someone using one. Oh, what fun it would be to squirt all the toys! She stole towards it and picked it up. Dear me, it *was* heavy! She ran at the surprised pink rabbit, pressed down the handle – and out gushed the soda water all over him!

"Ow! Ooh!" he shouted, in astonishment. "What is it! What is it! Amelia Jane, you ought to be ashamed of yourself!"

But she wasn't a bit ashamed. She was enjoying herself thoroughly! She ran after the teddy bear and soaked him with soda water too. She squirted lots over the clockwork mouse, and made him so wet that for two days his clockwork went wrong, and he couldn't be wound up. She squirted the pink rabbit again and he got into the waste-paper basket and couldn't get out, which worried him very much because he was so afraid that he would be thrown away the next day! Luckily, he wasn't.

"Amelia Jane is up to her tricks again," said the clockwork clown, frowning. "We shall have no peace at all. What shall we do?"

"Take away her key!" said the clockwork mouse.

"She hasn't one, silly!" said the curly-haired doll.

118

"Lock her in the cupboard!" said the teddy bear.

"She knows how to undo it from the inside," said the pink rabbit gloomily.

Nobody spoke for a whole minute. They were all thinking hard.

Then the clockwork clown gave a little laugh. "I know!" he said. "I've thought of an idea. It's quite simple, but it might work."

"What?" cried everyone.

"Let's polish Amelia Jane's shoes underneath and make them very, very slippery," said the clown. "Then, if she begins to run after us with soda water syphons or things like that, down she'll go!"

"But she won't like that," said the curly-haired doll, who was rather tender-hearted.

"Well, *we* don't like the tricks she plays on *us*!" said the teddy bear. "We'll do it, Clown! When she next takes her shoes off we'll polish them underneath till they are as slippery as glass!"

The very next night Amelia Jane took off her shoes because her feet were hot. She put the shoes into a corner and then danced round the playroom in her socks, enjoying herself. The clown picked up the shoes and ran away to the back of the toy cupboard with them. He had a tiny duster there, and a little bit of polish he had taken out of the polish jar when the playroom had been cleaned out.

Aha, Amelia Jane, you'll be sorry for all your tricks! The clown polished and rubbed, rubbed and polished. The soles of the shoes shone. They were as slippery as could be! The clown put them back and waited for Amelia Jane to put them on. This she very soon did, for she stepped on a pin and pricked her foot! She ran to put on her shoes. As she put them on, she thought out a naughty trick!

"I'll run after all the toys with that pin I trod on!" she thought. "Oooh! That will make them rush away into all the corners! What fun it will be to frighten them!"

She buttoned her shoes and took the nasty long pin. Then she stood up and looked round, her naughty black eyes gleaming. "I'll run after that fat little teddy bear!" she thought. So off she went, straight at the teddy bear, holding the pin out in front of her.

"Amelia Jane, put that pin down!" shouted the teddy bear in fright – but before Amelia Jane had taken three steps, her very, very slippery shoes slid along the ground and down she fell, bumpity-bump! She *was* surprised!

Up she got again and took a few more steps towards the teddy bear – but her shoes slipped and down she fell! Bumpity-bump!

"What's the matter with the carpet?" cried Amelia Jane, in a rage. "It keeps making me fall down!"

"Ha ha! ho ho!" laughed the toys. "Perhaps there is slippery magic about, Amelia Jane!"

"Oh, I believe you toys have something to do with it!" shouted the angry doll. Up she got and took the pin in her hand again. "I'll show you what happens to people who put slippery magic on the floor! Here comes my pin!"

She tried to run at the pink rabbit, who was laughing so much that pink tears ran all down his face. But down she went again, bumpity-bump — and oh my, the pin stuck into her knee! Yes, it really did — she fell on it!

How Amelia Jane squealed! How Amelia Jane wept! "Oh, the horrid pin! Oh, how it hurts!" she cried.

"Well, Amelia Jane, it serves you right," said the pink rabbit. "You were going to prick *us* with that pin and now it's pricked *you*! You know how it feels!"

Amelia Jane threw the pin away in a rage. The clown picked it up and threw it into the waste-paper basket. He wasn't going to have pins about the playroom!

Amelia Jane got up again. "I'm going to bandage my knee where the pin pricked it," she said. She ran to the toy cupboard – but before she was half-way there, her slippery shoes slid away beneath her – and down she sat with a dreadful bumpity-bumpity-bump!

The toys laughed. Amelia Jane cried bitterly. The curly-haired doll felt sorry for her. "Don't cry any more, Amelia Jane," she said. "Take your shoes off and you won't fall any more. We played a trick on you – but you can't complain because you have so often tricked *us*! You should not play jokes on other people if you can't take a joke yourself!"

Amelia Jane took her shoes off. She saw how the clown had polished them underneath, and she went very red. She knew quite well she could not grumble if people were unkind – because she too had been unkind.

"I'll try and be good, toys," she said, at last. "It's difficult for me, because I'm not a shop toy like you, so I haven't learnt good manners and nice ways. But I may be good one day!"

The toys thought it was nice of her to say all that. The curly-haired doll came to help her bandage her knee. She looked so funny that they didn't know whether to laugh or cry at her.

Amelia Jane did enjoy being fussed! She is as nice as can be to the toys now – but oh dear, oh dear, I do somehow feel perfectly certain it won't last long! I'll tell you if it doesn't.

# Brer Rabbit and
## the Bigger-Wigger

O ne night Brer Rabbit came to Brer Terrapin's house looking mighty scared. Brer Terrapin let him in and closed the door.

"What's sent you out into the night?" said old Brer Terrapin. "You're shaking like a leaf in the wind, Brer Rabbit. Who's after you?"

"It's Brer Wolf and Brer Fox," said Brer Rabbit. "I was a-sitting in my kitchen, eating my dinner, when I suddenly saw Brer Wolf's face looking in at my window – and when I ran into the bedroom, there was Brer Fox's face looking in there!"

"So you shot out of your house and came here," said Brer Terrapin. "Well, you've been playing such pranks on them lately, Brer Rabbit, that it's no wonder they're after you!"

"Perhaps they're on the way here to *your* house," said Brer Rabbit, after a bit. "Was that a leaf a-stirring – or was it a footfall?"

"It was the fire crackling," said Brer Terrapin. "Now you just listen to me, Brer Rabbit. I guess those two will follow you here – and I don't want a fight in *my* house, I only cleaned it up today. I've thought of a plan."

"What is it?" said Brer Rabbit. "You'll have to be quick, Brer Terrapin!"

"I'm going out," said Brer Terrapin. "And I'll scout around. If I see Brer Fox and Brer Wolf come along here, look out for some more visitors, will you?"

"What do you mean?" said Brer Rabbit, but Brer Terrapin only grinned at him.

126

"My door doesn't lock," he said, "so look out, Brer Rabbit. You'll have to let Brer Fox and Brer Wolf in, if they come. But be careful you don't let any other visitors in, see?"

"You're talking in riddles," said Brer Rabbit crossly – but Brer Terrapin had crawled slowly out of the house, taking his heavy shell with him.

No sooner had he gone than a bang came at the door. Brer Rabbit trembled. He didn't say a word, but got under the bed. The door swung open and in came Brer Wolf and Brer Fox.

"Nobody's at home," said Brer Fox.

"Oh, yes – somebody is," said Brer Wolf, and pointed to where one of Brer Rabbit's hind legs peeped out from under the bed. He pounced on it and dragged out Brer Rabbit, who wriggled like a snake.

"Oho! So you ran to Brer Terrapin's! We reckoned you would," said Brer Wolf. "Now – just you set a pot on the fire and heat some water. We'll have you for our supper, and maybe if Brer Terrapin comes back home we'll ask him to share it!"

"You leave me alone," said Brer Rabbit. "I've done you no harm!"

"Who hid behind the tree and called us names?" said Brer Fox.

"Who pelted us with conkers? Who poured water down our chimney?" said Brer Wolf. "Well, we've got you this time, Brer Rabbit, and we're going to keep you. Now – fill that pot."

BANG, BANG!

Everyone jumped. Brer Rabbit, too.

"Somebody at the door," said Brer Fox. "No, don't you go and open it, Brer

Rabbit. We're not letting you scamper away." He raised his voice and shouted, "Who's there?"

"I'm one of the Bigger-Wiggers," said a strange voice. "And I'm hungry. *Ooooomph, ooooomph!*"

"A Bigger-Wigger! What's that?" said Brer Fox in alarm. "What a horrible voice!"

"What does a hungry Bigger-Wigger eat?" called Brer Rabbit. This must be one of the visitors that Brer Terrapin had talked about! What a joke!

"I eat foxes, bears, wolves and lions," said the voice. "*Oooomph, ooomph, ooomph!*"

"Could you eat a rabbit?" yelled Brer Fox.

"Rabbit? No! They're nothing but skin and bone," said the voice. "Give me a nice fat *wolf!*"

Brer Rabbit opened his mouth to answer, and Brer Wolf at once put his paw over it. "Don't you dare to say there's a wolf here," he muttered.

Then Brer Fox answered the voice at the door. "No. There's no wolf here. Go away, Bigger-Wigger."

"I'm hunnnnn-grrrrry!" said the voice. "We're *all* hungry. *Oooomph!*"

Brer Fox and Brer Wolf heard footsteps going away and felt most relieved. Brer Fox got up to lock the door, but there was no key.

"Suppose another Bigger-Wigger comes?" he said in alarm. "It could open the door if it wanted to. What a good thing *that* one didn't try!"

"Oh – no more Bigger-Wiggers will come," said Brer Rabbit, hiding a smile.

But just at that very moment a weird sound came to their ears. "*Plink! Plonk! Plooooonk!*"

"What's that?" cried Brer Fox, and clutched Brer Wolf so suddenly that he almost made him jump out of his skin.

"Another Bigger-Wigger!" said Brer Wolf. "And don't clutch at me like that, Brer Fox. It felt as if you were a Bigger-Wigger! Ssh!"

Another knock came at the door. BLAM! BLAM! BLAM!

"Who's there?" demanded Brer Rabbit.

"A Bigger-Wigger," said a hollow voice. "And I'm hungry. *Plink! Plonk! Ploooonk!*"

Brer Rabbit knew who *that* was! It was Mr Benjamin Ram and his fiddle. Brer Terrapin must have fetched him.

"What a horrible noise," said Brer Fox, trembling. Another knock came at the door. BLAM!

"Let me in! I'm hungry. I want a fox or a bear or a lion to eat," said the voice.

"Would a wolf do?" yelled Brer Rabbit before Brer Wolf could stop him. A pleased, gurgling noise came from outside the door, and then a fumbling as if the Bigger-Wigger was trying to find the handle.

"There's no wolf here! Go away!" yelled Brer Wolf in a panic.

"What a pity!" said the voice, and then footsteps began to walk away.

There came the sound of *"Plink! Plonk! Ploooonk!"* again, and Brer Rabbit grinned as he pictured old Mr Ram pulling at the strings of his fiddle.

"Hadn't you better get home before any more Bigger-Wiggers come?" said Brer Rabbit to Brer Wolf and Brer Fox. "They seem to be after foxes and wolves. Thank goodness they don't want rabbits."

"Maybe they don't – but *we* do," said Brer Fox, making a grab at Brer Rabbit. "Into that pot you'll go, Bigger-Wiggers or no Bigger-Wiggers!"

"Wait! Listen! *What's that?*" cried Brer Rabbit. "Look – at the window! Is it a Bigger-Wigger? Hadn't you better blow out the candle before he sees there's a fox and a wolf here?"

In a panic Brer Fox blew out the candle. Yes, there was a scuffling noise at the window. Brer Rabbit smiled to himself in the darkness – that sounded like old Brer Terrapin again. *Scuffle, scuffle, scuffle. Oooomph! Ooooooomph!*

*OOOO-OOMPH! OOO-OOOMPH!*

While Brer Fox and Brer Wolf clutched each other in the darkness, Brer Rabbit crept to the door. He opened it and slipped out. He shut it with a bang that made Brer Fox and Brer Wolf dive under the bed together.

"The Bigger-Wigger," they yelled. But no Bigger-Wigger came in. In fact, there wasn't another sound. They lay under the bed for a while and then came out and lit the candle, looking round fearfully.

"No Bigger-Wigger," said Brer Fox, with a huge sigh of relief.

"And no Brer Rabbit either! He's gone!" said Brer Wolf, in a rage. "Just when we had him nicely, too – and the pot's boiling ready to cook him!"

*Blam-blam-blam!* Brer Fox yelped in fright. Who was that at the door now? It opened – and in came old Brer Terrapin, looking just the same as ever.

"Who's this in my house?" he said to

Brer Fox and Brer Wolf. "Who comes visiting when I'm not at home? Get out, or I'll call the Bigger-Wiggers I've just seen in the wood!"

"No. Don't do that. We're going," said Brer Wolf. And they went, Brer Fox clutching at Brer Wolf in case they met a Bigger-Wigger.

Brer Terrapin laughed till his shell almost cracked. "You can come in, Brer Rabbit!" he called. "And Mr Ram, too. We'll have a nice supper together. The pot's boiling!"

In came old Brer Rabbit and Mr Benjamin Ram with his fiddle. "Thanks for your help, Mr Ram," said Brer Rabbit. "I'm glad Brer Terrapin fetched you and your fiddle – it scared Brer Fox and Brer Wolf like anything!"

There they sit in front of the fire, with a nice supper boiling in the pot. Mr Ram's got his fiddle and he's pulling at the strings. Listen! *Plink! Plonk! Ploooonk!*

## The clever little cat

John and Shirley had a little cat. They had had him since he was a kitten, and they called him Zebby, because he was striped like a zebra.

Zebby was a clever little thing. He hadn't grown very big, but he was strong and healthy. He mewed with joy whenever he saw John and Shirley, for they loved him and were kind to him.

They taught Zebby quite a lot of tricks. The little cat could rattle the handle of a door by standing on his hind legs. He could play hide-and-seek with the children. He could sit up and beg just like a dog.

He rubbed himself against the

136

children's legs, and purred when he sat on their knees.

"He sounds like the mowing machine!" said Shirley, tickling Zebby round the ears to make him purr more loudly.

But Mummy wasn't quite so pleased with Zebby. "He's a little thief!" she said. "If the food cupboard door is left open he creeps inside and takes whatever he can! And he makes such a noise at night, too, if he's left out. He won't come in when he's called – so he has to be left out – and then he yowls the place down!"

"Oh, Mummy! Zebby's a darling!" said John, and picked up the purring little cat.

"Well, darling or not, Zebby will have to go to another home if he doesn't stop stealing!" said Mummy.

"Do you hear that, Zebby?" asked Shirley. "You must stop at once, because we couldn't bear to lose you. Come and play ball with us."

Zebby ran across the grass with John and Shirley. He was very good with a ball. Whenever he found one he rolled it along with his paw, pretended it was a mouse, jumped at it, sidled all round it, and then set it rolling again. There was nothing he loved quite so much as a ball.

For two days Zebby was very good. Then Mummy and Daddy were going to have a tennis-party, and Mummy bought some salmon to make sandwiches – and, will you believe it, Zebby smelt out that salmon, watched till the food cupboard door was open, and walked in! He hid under the shelf when he heard Cook coming, but as soon as she was out of the way, Zebby jumped up on the shelf and began to eat that nice pink salmon!

So, when Cook went to fetch it for the sandwiches, there was no salmon to be seen, except a bone on the plate, licked quite bare!

"That cat again!" cried Cook, and went to tell Mummy, who was changing into her tennis things. She was very angry.

"You'll have to open the potted meat, Cook," she said. "The bad little cat! I won't keep him in the house a week longer!"

She hunted for Zebby to tell him off, but the little cat had run away to hide. Zebby knew quite well he had done wrong, and he wanted to find somewhere safe.

He ran upstairs. He went into the loft. He jumped out of the loft window on to the roof, and found a nice warm place by the chimney. He curled himself up and went to sleep. Nobody would find him there!

Cook made some potted meat sandwiches. Mummy and Daddy went out to put up the net, and the children tipped out nine new balls on to the green lawn. The guests began to arrive.

John and Shirley were ball-boys. They hunted for the balls that ran into the bushes or bounced over the net into the long orchard grass. They talked about naughty little Zebby.

"I do wish Mummy would let us keep Zebby," said Shirley. "He's been ours for three years now, and he's the nicest little cat I know."

"I wonder where he is," said John. "He's very clever at hiding himself when he's naughty!"

They soon knew where he was! One of the guests hit a ball very wildly and it went spinning up, up, up to the roof of the house! It fell right on Zebby, who was asleep by the chimney, and he woke with a loud squeak of fright. The ball dropped down the roof to the gutter and stayed there.

"There's Zebby!" said Shirley. "Up on the roof! That ball must have woken him up! Zebby, Zebby, Zebby! Come on down!"

But Zebby didn't. He lay there sleepily watching the tennis. Soon another ball flew up on the roof and stuck in the gutter. Zebby watched it with much interest. He got up and strolled down the sloping roof to the gutter.

Mummy was sorry that the balls had gone there because nobody could get them, and they would go rotten in the next rainstorm. But Zebby began to play with the two balls, trying to get them out of the wet gutter.

One ball came out and dropped down to the ground with a big bounce. The children gave a shriek of delight. "Mummy, Zebby's getting the balls off the roof for you!"

Zebby scooped out the second one, but before he could play with it, it dropped to the ground, of course! Everybody laughed and cheered.

"Two good balls saved!" said Daddy. "Thank you, Zebby!"

Zebby waited up on the roof for more balls. Soon one came – and then another – for the court was really too near the house, and many a time balls had been lost in the gutters. Zebby waited for the balls, and wherever they happened to stick he ran to them, and pawed them until he got them free. Then down they fell to the ground.

"What a clever little cat!" cried all the guests. "You must be proud of him! How useful he will be at tennis-parties, too — you will never lose balls in the gutter again!"

Well, Mummy and Daddy did begin to feel very proud of Zebby!

"He's saved no end of new balls for us today," said Daddy. "Can't we keep the food cupboard door shut, Mummy, and keep Zebby?"

"I really think we'd better try," said Mummy — and how John and Shirley cheered! So a spring was fixed to the food cupboard door, and whenever it was left open by mistake the door closed itself — so Zebby could never get inside to steal again.

He's still living with John and Shirley, and when I go there to play tennis I love to see him sitting on the roof waiting

for the balls. Sometimes we send one up there just for fun – we do love to see him paw it out of the gutter and send it down to the ground once more! Isn't he clever?

## The witch's cat

Old Dame Kirri was a witch. You could tell she was because she had bright green eyes. She was a good witch though, and spent most of her time making good spells to help people who were ill or unhappy.

She lived in Toppling Cottage, which was just like its name, and looked exactly as if it was going to topple over. But it was kept up by strong magic, and not a brick had fallen, although the cottage was five hundred years old.

At the back of the cottage was the witch's garden. Round it ran a very, very high wall, taller than the tallest man.

"I like a high wall. It keeps people

from peeping and prying," said old Witch Kirri. "In my garden I grow a lot of strange and powerful herbs. I don't want people to see them and steal them. I won't have people making spells from my magic herbs – they might make bad ones."

The witch had a cat. It was black and big, and had green eyes very like the witch's. Its name was Cinder-Boy.

Cinder-Boy helped the witch with her spells. He was really a remarkably clever cat. He knew how to sit exactly in the middle of a chalk ring without moving, whilst Kirri the witch danced round and sang spells. He knew how to go out and collect dew-drops in the moonlight. He took a special little silver cup for that, and never spilt a drop.

He never drank milk. He liked tea, made as strong as the witch made for herself. Sometimes he would sit and sip his tea and purr, and the witch would sip *her* tea and purr, too. It was funny to see them.

Cinder-Boy loved to sleep in the walled-in garden. He knew all the flowers and herbs there. No weeds were allowed to grow. Cinder-Boy scratched them all up.

But one day he came to a small plant growing at the foot of the wall. It had leaves like a rose-tree. It had pale pink flowers, with a mass of yellow stamens in the middle. It smelt very sweet.

"What flower are you?" said Cinder-Boy. "You smell rather like a rose."

"Well, that's just what I am," said the plant. "I'm a wild rose."

"How did you get here?" said Cinder-Boy, surprised.

"A bird dropped a seed," said the wild rose. "But I don't like being here, black cat."

"My name is Cinder-Boy," said the witch's cat. "Why don't you like being here? It is a very nice place to be."

"Well, I feel shut in," said the wild rose. "I'm not very large. If I was taller than the wall I could grow up into the air, and see over the top. I don't like being down here at the bottom, shut in."

"Well, grow tall then," said Cinder-Boy. "I can give you a spell to make your stems nice and long, if you like. Then you can reach up to the top of the wall and look over. There's a nice view there, I can tell you."

"Oh, would you do that?" said the wild rose in delight. "Thank you!"

So Cinder-Boy went off to get a spell to make the stems of the wild rose grow very long. He soon found one. It was in a small blue bottle, and he poured it into a watering-can. The spell was blue, too.

Then he watered the wild rose with the spell, and it began to work almost at once. In two or three days the stems of the wild rose plant had grown quite high into the air.

"Go on growing. You will soon be at the top of the wall!" said Cinder-Boy. So the wild rose went on making its stems longer and longer, hoping to get to the very top of the wall.

But when Cinder-Boy next strolled out into the garden to see how it was getting on, what a shock he had! Every single stem was bent over and lay sprawling over the grass!

"Why, what has happened?" said Cinder-Boy, waving his tail in surprise.

"My stalks grew tall, but they didn't grow strong," said the wild rose, sadly. "Just as I reached the top of the wall, they all flopped over and fell down. They are not strong enough to bear their own weight."

"Well, how do plants with weak stems manage to climb high then?" said Cinder-Boy, puzzled. "Runner beans grow high and they have very weak stems. Sweet peas grow high, and they have weak stems too. I'll go and see how they do it."

So off he went, for the witch grew both in the garden. He soon came back.

"The beans twine their stalks around poles," he said, "and the sweet peas grow little green fingers, called tendrils, which catch hold of things, and they pull themselves up high like that. Can't you do that?"

The wild rose couldn't. It didn't know how to. Its stems wouldn't twist themselves, however much it tried to make them do so. And it couldn't grow a tendril at all.

"Well, we must think of another way," said the cat.

"Cinder-Boy, how do *you* get up to the top of the wall?" asked the wild rose. "You are often up there in the sun. I see you. Well, how do *you* get to the top?"

"I run up the trees," said Cinder-Boy. "Do you see the young fruit trees near you? Well, I run up those to the top of the wall. I use my claws to help me. I dig them into the bark of the trees, and hold on with them."

He showed the wild rose his big curved claws. "I can put them in or out as I like," he said. "They are very useful claws."

151

The wild rose thought they were too. "If I grew claws like that I could easily climb up the fruit trees, right through them to the top, and then I'd be waving at the top of the wall," it said. "Can't you get me some claws like yours, Cinder-Boy?"

The cat blinked his green eyes and thought hard. "I know what I could do," he said. "I could ask the witch Kirri, my mistress, to make some magic claws that would grow on you. I'll ask her today. In return you must promise to grow her some lovely scarlet hip berries that she can trim her hats and bonnets with in the autumn."

"Oh, I will, I will," promised the wild rose. So Cinder-Boy went off to the witch Kirri and asked her for what he wanted.

She grumbled a little. "It is difficult to make claws," she said. "Very difficult. You will have to help me, Cinder-Boy. You will have to sit in the middle of a blue ring of chalk, and put out all your claws at once, whilst I sing a magic song. Don't be scared at what happens."

Cinder-Boy went to sit in the middle of a chalk ring that the witch drew in the middle of the garden. He stuck out all his claws as she commanded.

She danced round with her broomstick, singing such a magic song that Cinder-Boy felt quite scared. Then a funny thing happened.

His claws fell out on to the ground with a clatter – and they turned red or green as they fell. He looked at his paws and saw new ones growing. Then those fell out, too. How very, very strange!

Soon there was quite a pile of claws on the ground. Then the witch stopped singing and dancing, and rubbed out the ring of chalk.

"You can come out now, Cinder-Boy," she said. "The magic is finished."

Cinder-Boy collected all the red and green claws. They were strong and curved and sharp. He took them to the bottom of the garden, and came to the wild rose.

"I've got claws for you!" he said. "The witch Kirri did some strong magic. Look, here they are. I'll press each one into your stems, till you have claws all down them. Then I'll say a growing spell, and they will grow into you properly, and belong to you."

So Cinder-Boy did that, and the wild

rose felt the cat-claws growing firmly into the long stems.

"Now," said Cinder-Boy, in excitement, "now you will be able to climb up through the fruit tree, wild rose. I will help you at first."

So Cinder-Boy took the wild rose stems, all set with claws, and pushed them up into the little fruit tree that grew near by. The claws took hold of the bark and held on firmly. Soon all the stems were climbing up high through the little fruit tree, the claws digging themselves into the trunk and the branches.

The wild rose grew higher. It pulled itself up by its new claws. It was soon at the top of the wall! It could see right over it to the big world beyond.

"Now I'm happy!" said the wild rose to Cinder-Boy. "Come and sit up here on the wall beside me. Let us look at the big world together. Oh, Cinder-Boy, it is lovely up here. I am not shut in any longer. Thank you for my claws.

I do hope I shall go on growing them now."

It did. And it grew beautiful scarlet berries in the autumn, for witch Kirri's winter bonnets. You should see how pretty they are when she trims them with the rose hips!

Ever since that day the wild roses have grown cats' claws all down their stems, sometimes green and sometimes red or pink. They use them to climb with. Have you seen them? If you haven't, do go and look. It will surprise you to see cats' claws growing out of a plant!

It was a good idea of Cinder-Boy's, wasn't it?

# The wizard and
# the Rubdubs

Once upon a time little Prince Philomel was on his travels round Fairyland, when he suddenly saw a curious sight. Coming towards him was a crowd of little people, all looking very miserable. None of them wore hats, and they all had heads as bald as eggs.

One of them was dressed much more grandly than the others and Philomel spoke to him.

"Who are you, and what's the matter with you all?" he asked.

"We are the Rubdubs," answered the little man, with tears trickling down his cheeks. "I am the King of the Rubdubs, and my palace isn't very far away. A great misfortune has befallen us, as you can see."

"Tell me about it," said Philomel.

"Well, we were all out walking this morning," began the little King, "and we met a very kind-looking wizard. He invited us into his cottage, and offered us some lovely coloured sweets out of a tin. We each took one, and no sooner had we swallowed it than what do you think happened?"

"What?" asked Philomel.

"Why, every hair on our heads fell out!" wept the little King, and all the Rubdubs wept too, so that a big puddle began to form on the path.

"Well, but didn't you tell the wizard to put your hair back for you at once?" asked Philomel in surprise.

"Of *course* we did!" said the King. "But all he said was — 'Pay me a hundred gold crowns and I will show you how to get your hair back.' Well I haven't got even fifty gold crowns,

because it is expensive to be a King nowadays, and besides, I spent all my money on my palace, which is a very beautiful one. So we had to come away bald!"

He cried big tears again, and Philomel wished he had wellingtons on.

"Never mind," he said. "I'll put things right for you. I'll go straight to that rogue of a wizard now."

"Oh, be careful, be careful," begged the Rubdub King. "You'll come back bald or something, really you will! He's a wicked creature, that wizard!"

But Philomel only laughed. He knew what the Rubdubs didn't know – and that was that no spell of any sort could harm him, for a witch had once rubbed him with fresh elderflower under the new moon, and that kept all harm from him.

He went along to where the Rubdubs had told him the wizard lived. Sure enough, he soon saw a cottage. Someone was peering from the window and, as soon as Philomel drew near, the wizard came out of the front door.

"A nice morning, a very nice morning," he said to Philomel, smiling very broadly.

"It is," said Philomel. "What a lovely place this is to live in! How lucky you are to have your cottage in this wood!"

"Indeed I am," said the wizard. "But won't you come in for a moment and see it? I have many curious things inside which I'm sure you'd like to see."

"Thank you," said Philomel, and he followed the grinning wizard inside the hut.

"Sit down, sit down," said the wizard. He went to a cupboard and opened it. He took out a large tin and went across to Philomel.

"Have a sweet?" he asked. "They're most delicious. I bought them from an old witch yesterday. They make you feel lovely."

"Thank you very much," said Philomel, knowing quite well that the sweets were the same as those that had made all the little Rubdubs bald. He popped it into his mouth and crunched it. It certainly tasted delicious. The wizard watched him closely, and when Philomel's hair did not fall off, he looked very puzzled.

Then Philomel did a bit of pretending. He jumped up from his chair and clapped his hands with joy.

"Oh!" he cried. "That was a magic sweet! Oh! I am full of the most powerful magic now! I know things I never knew before! I can read the stars! I can hear the grass growing! I know all the languages in the world!"

"What!" cried the wizard. "Can you really? I must have given you the wrong sweet!"

"Oh, give me more, give me more!" cried Philomel, enjoying himself very much. He snatched four or five from the tin and crunched them up loudly.

Then he danced round the room.

"I know more magic than anyone else in the world! The sweets are telling me all the secrets of Fairyland! I am getting more powerful every minute! Oh, give me more of those wonderful sweets!"

He snatched at the tin again, but the wizard pushed him away.

"*No!*" he said. "I shall eat the rest myself! I'm not going to have you taking all the magic like this. I'd no idea I'd got such wonderful sweets. All the top ones were quite different. They simply made people bald!"

He greedily filled his mouth full of the sweets and crunched them up. Then he waited to feel the magic coming but nothing happened — but wait a minute — yes, something *was* happening! What was this tumbling down on the floor? Oh my, oh my, it was the wizard's fine, thick hair!

"I've eaten the wrong sweets! Oh, oh! I'm bald like the Rubdubs!" he cried. "Oh, what a dreadful thing, for I'm going out to tea this afternoon, and how can I go bald? Oh, I must quickly find a spell to put it right again."

Philomel pretended to be very sorry for him. He helped him to look through all his magic books until he had found how to get his hair back again.

"I must make a mixture of new honey, six dewdrops, the scent of a violet, some silk from a spider's web, some bottled moonlight and stir it all up with an owl's feather," said the wizard in a trembling voice. "Oh dear, oh dear! Well, it's easy enough to get the first four things, but I haven't very much bottled moonlight left, I'm afraid."

He took down a bottle and shook it.

"Only just enough," he said. He quickly made the mixture, poured in the silver moonlight, and stirred it all up with an owl's feather.

"Now if you'll help me," he said to Philomel, "I shall soon be all right again, with all my hair back safely. I must kneel down in a chalk circle, close my eyes and count fifty. Then you must pour the mixture over my head, and all my hair will grow again as thick and as long as before."

Philomel took the bottle with the mixture in, and waited until the wizard was kneeling down with his eyes closed, counting fifty. Then, very quietly, Philomel stole out of the door, and ran back to the Rubdubs as fast as he could.

"Quick, quick!" he said. "Kneel down, shut your eyes and count fifty. I'm just going to draw a chalk circle round you, and then pour this magic stuff over your heads!"

In a second all the Rubdubs were on their knees, counting. When they came to fifty, Philomel poured a little of the moonlight mixture on each of their little bald heads, and sure enough the hair sprouted again and grew long and thick and curly! How delighted the

Rubdubs were, and how they crowded round Philomel and begged him to come and stay at their palace.

Suddenly there came a noise like an angry bull, and the wizard burst upon them, his eyes flashing wildly.

"You've taken my mixture!" he cried. "I waited and waited for you to pour it, and you were gone! Oh, you've used it all on those wretched little Rubdubs! Oh, you thief, you robber!"

Philomel laughed.

"You're the thief and the robber!" he said. "You took away the Rubdubs' hair, and I gave it back to them. Here you are, catch! There's your precious bottle back, but it's empty!"

The wizard caught it and hurried away. He managed to squeeze two drops from it and rubbed them on his bald head, but as only four long hairs grew, he looked funnier than ever.

Still, as Philomel said, it really *did* serve him right!

# *The poor little sparrow*

Every morning Ronnie and Sylvia put out crumbs for the birds, and a little bowl of water. The birds always knew when the children were going to throw out the food, and they came flocking down to wait.

"Chirrup-chirrup!" said all the sparrows, dressed in brown.

"Tirry-lee, tirry-lee!" sang the robin in his creamy voice.

"Fizz, splutter, wheeee!" chattered the starlings in their funny voices.

"Pink, pink!" the pink-chested chaffinch shouted.

"Aren't they lovely?" said the children, as they threw out the crumbs and some crusts from the toast. "They really are friendly little things."

The children knew all the birds, though it was difficult to tell one sparrow from another. They knew the smallest one of all, though, because he had one white feather in his tail, and that made him look rather odd.

One day the little sparrow flew down with the others, but it couldn't seem to stand on the ground properly. It fell over – then tried to stand upright again – and then fell over again.

"Look at the poor little sparrow," said Sylvia, who was very tender-hearted. "What's the matter with it? It can't stand."

"It's hurt its leg," said Ronnie. "Oh, Sylvia – I believe its leg is broken. Can you see?"

Sylvia went slowly closer to the birds. They did not mind, for they trusted the two children. "Oh, Ronnie, you are right," she said. "Its leg is broken in two. Whatever are we to do?"

Now the poor little sparrow had that

morning been caught by a cat, but had managed to get away. Its little leg had been broken, and the tiny creature did not know why it could not stand properly, nor why it was in pain. It had joined the other birds as usual for its breakfast, but it could not eat, for it felt too ill.

Suddenly it fell right over and lay on the grass. Its eyes closed. Sylvia picked it up gently and put its soft little head against her cheek.

"Poor little sparrow," she said. "It says in the Bible that God sees every sparrow that falls, so I expect He saw you too, and hoped I would pick you up. Well, I have – but I don't know what to do to make you better."

But her mother knew. As soon as she saw the little bird she took out the old, empty, canary's cage and put the sparrow on to some clean sand at the bottom of the cage.

"It has had a shock," said their mother. "It will come awake soon, and will be all right. Oh, look! Its leg is broken!"

"How can we mend it?" asked Sylvia, almost in tears.

"Well," said her mother, "if *we* break our legs the doctor sets the bone in the right position, and then ties it to something that will keep it straight till the broken bone joins together and grows properly again. What can we tie to the sparrow's tiny leg to keep it straight?"

"A match – a match!" cried Ronnie, and he emptied some out of a box.

"That's a good idea," said Mummy. She gently picked up the sparrow, whose eyes were still closed, and laid it on the table. Then she tried to set the poor little leg straight. With strands of silk she fastened the straight matchstick to the thin, small leg. It looked very strange – but now the broken leg was straight again.

"Oh, Mummy," said Sylvia joyfully, "you've done it so nicely. When the bone joins again, the leg will be quite all right, won't it?"

"I hope so," said her mother, putting the sparrow into the cage and shutting the door. "We shall keep the tiny thing in here, and feed it until the leg is quite right, and then it shall go free again."

When the sparrow opened its eyes, it was surprised to find itself in a cage. Its leg still felt strange, but it now no longer fell over, because the matchstick supported it. The little bird flew to a perch and chirruped.

Ronnie gave it some seed. Sylvia gave it a mixture of potato and breadcrumbs, and the sparrow was simply delighted. It had a little dish of water for a bath and another dish to drink from, set at the side of the big cage. At first it fluttered its wings against the bars of the cage to get out, for it hated not being free. But, as it still did not feel very well, it soon gave up struggling and sat contentedly on a

perch, feeding and bathing whenever it wanted to.

The leg healed quickly. It was marvellous to see it. The skin joined nicely, and the broken bones seemed to grow together at once.

"I think we might let our little sparrow fly away now," said their mother one day. "I am sure his leg is all right."

"Are you going to take the matchstick off now?" asked Sylvia.

"Yes," said her mother. So she took hold of the half-frightened bird, and carefully and gently took away the silk binding from the leg and match. The match fell off – and the little leg was as straight and strong as ever.

"We've mended its leg! We've mended its leg!" shouted the children in delight. "You aren't a poor little sparrow any more. Fly away, fly away!"

The sparrow gave a chirrup and flew straight out of the window. How glad it was to be out of the cage! It flew into the trees, and chirruped so loudly that all the other sparrows came round to hear what it had to say.

Now you would not think that a small sparrow could possibly help the children in anything, would you? And yet, a few weeks later, a very strange thing happened.

Ronnie and Sylvia had some glass marbles, the prettiest things you ever saw. They were blue and green and pink, and had white lines curving through them. Ronnie and Sylvia were very proud of them, for they had belonged to their daddy.

"You can't get marbles like these nowadays," said Daddy. "Take care of them."

Well, Ronnie and Sylvia took them to play with in the fields, and there they met David, a big rough boy whom none of the children liked. When he saw the marbles he came up.

"Give me those," he said, "and I'll give you these reins of mine."

"No, thank you," said Ronnie, gathering his marbles up quickly. But he wasn't quick enough. David grabbed some of them and ran off laughing. Sylvia and Ronnie went after him.

"They are *our* marbles!" shouted Ronnie. "Give them back, David!"

"I'll put them somewhere and you take them," called back David – and what do you suppose he did with them? Why, the horrid boy dropped them all into a hole in a tree. Then he ran off, giggling.

Ronnie and Sylvia ran to the tree. They tried to slip their small hands into the hole but they couldn't. The hole was too small.

"We can't get our marbles out," said Sylvia. "They're gone. Oh, that horrid boy!"

"Chirrup!" said a cheerful little voice nearby. The children looked up. It was their little sparrow. They knew it was the same one because of the white feather in his tail.

"I wish *you* could get our marbles," sighed Ronnie. "Your foot is quite small enough to go into the hole, Sparrow."

"Chirrup!" said the sparrow – and what do you think he did? Why, he flew to the hole, and instead of putting in his foot, he put the whole of himself in. Yes, he quite disappeared into that little hole – but not for long.

He popped up again, head-first – and in his beak he held a green marble. He dropped it on to the ground and disappeared into the hole once more. Up he came, with a blue marble this time. The children were so astonished that they didn't even pick up the marbles.

The little sparrow fetched every single marble out of the hole before he flew off with a last cheerful chirrup. Then the children picked them up, and went racing home to tell their mother the strange and lovely happening.

"How very extraordinary!" she said. "It must be put into a story, for everyone will love to read about the poor little sparrow that did such a kind thing. It just shows what friends we can make, if only we are kind to even the smallest things."

So here is the story – and I do hope you enjoyed it.

# The tale of Jig and Jog

One day Jig and Jog, the two brownies who lived in Hollyhock Cottage, made up their minds to give a party.

"It shall be a birthday party," said Jig. "Then everyone will bring us presents. Won't that be nice, Jog?"

"Yes!" said Jog, rubbing his horny little hands in glee. "Ha! Presents of cakes! And sweets! And all kinds of exciting things!"

"We will give our party on November the fourteenth," said Jig. "We will send out the invitation cards now."

"Who shall come to the party?" said Jog.

"Well, we will ask Prickles the

hedgehog," said Jig. "He makes beautiful cakes. He might bring us one. We will put on our invitation cards that it is a birthday party. Then he will know he must bring a present."

"Who else shall come?" asked Jog.

"Well, Slinky the snake would be a good person to ask," said Jig, "and so would Slow-One the toad; and his cousin, Hoppity, the frog. Oh, and don't you think we could ask that bird who plays hide-and-seek so well – what's his name, now?"

"You mean the cuckoo," said Jog. "Yes, we will ask him too; and we will ask Dozy the little dormouse, for he is a generous fellow, and might even bring us a present each, instead of one between us."

The two brownies made out their list and then wrote out their invitation cards.

"Please come to a birthday party at Hollyhock Cottage on November the fourteenth, at four o'clock", they wrote on each card. Then they posted all the cards in the pillar-box at the end of the road, and waited for the answers.

The postman, Floppy the rabbit, took the cards and went to deliver them. He knew where Prickles the hedgehog lived, in a cosy hole in the sunny bankside of the hedge. He slipped the card into the hole. He knew where Slinky the snake lived too – in the old hollow tree in the middle of the wood. He climbed up and dropped the card down into the hole. He was a very good postman.

Then Floppy took Slow-One's card, and went to a big stone by the pond. He knew Slow-One the toad lived there. He pushed the card under the stone and left it. Hoppity the frog lived in the pond. Floppy waited until a stickleback came up to the top of the water and asked him to take the card to Hoppity. The fish caught the card neatly in its mouth and swam off with it.

"Now there's the card for the cuckoo,"

said Floppy Rabbit to himself. "Well, he was always sitting in that big beech tree, calling 'cuckoo' to everyone, so I'll put his card there. He is sure to see it if he sits there again."

Floppy had only one card left now – and that was for Dozy the dormouse. Floppy knew quite well where Dozy was living. He was in a cosy hole deep down in the roots of the big fir tree at the edge of the wood, not far from Floppy's own burrow. So, being a sensible rabbit, Floppy left that card till last, stuffed it into Dozy's hole, and then slipped into his own burrow for a rest and a cup of carrot tea.

Jig and Jog waited impatiently for the answers to their invitations. But none came! It was most extraordinary. Jig and Jog were puzzled. And then Jig thought he knew why. They had not put on the cards that they wanted an answer! So perhaps all their guests had thought they need not reply. Well, it didn't matter. The two brownies felt quite sure they would all turn up at the party on the right day – each bringing a very nice present!

They began to get ready for the party. They each had a new suit made, a red one for Jig and a blue one for Jog. They made a batch of chocolate cakes and a batch of ginger ones. They made strawberry jam sandwiches. They put out a clean cloth and arranged chairs all round their small table.

"We said four o'clock on the invitation cards," said Jig, when the day came. "It's half-past three now. Are we quite, quite ready, Jog?"

"Well, we've put on our new suits, and we've laid the table and put out the cakes and sandwiches and arranged the chairs," said Jog. "Yes, we are quite ready. I wonder who will come first!"

"And I wonder what everyone will bring us," said Jig. "It's a good thing we told everyone it was a birthday party, so that we can get presents."

Four o'clock came – but nobody

walked up the garden path. How strange! Quarter-past four and still no guests! Half-past four – five o'clock! Where could everyone be? There were the cakes and the sandwiches – but no guests to eat them. Jig and Jog looked as if they were going to cry!

They went down the garden path and looked up and down the road. Only Dame Chippy was there, coming along with the washing. When she saw their sad faces she stopped.

"What's the matter?" she asked.

"Well," said Jig mournfully, "we sent out invitations to Prickles, Slinky, Slow-One, Hoppity, the cuckoo and Dozy to come to a birthday party today – and nobody's come – and we shan't get any presents."

"Don't you know that you never tell anyone a party is a *birthday* party?" said Dame Chippy, shocked. "Why, that's just asking for presents, and nobody with good manners does that. It serves you right that nobody has come."

"But *why* haven't they come?" wailed Jog.

"If you think hard you'll know," said Dame Chippy, with a grin.

Jig and Jog thought hard – but they didn't know. Do you? Dame Chippy had to tell them.

"You are two silly creatures," she said. "Don't you know that Prickles the hedgehog always finds a hole for himself in the winter and sleeps the cold days away? Don't you know that Slinky the snake hates the cold and hides in a hollow tree fast asleep until the spring comes? And Slow-One the toad is never awake in the winter, sillies! He is sound asleep under his big stone – and his cousin, Hoppity the frog, is hidden in the mud at the bottom of the pond! As for the cuckoo, he has left the land months ago. He always goes south for the winter to find warmth and food."

"What about Dozy?" asked Jig in a small voice.

"He sleeps more soundly than any of

them!" said Dame Chippy. "He's snoring in the roots of the old fir tree! Well, well, well – no wonder you have no guests and no birthday presents! It serves you right for being so stupid and greedy!"

"Oh, all our cards were wasted, and all our cakes will be wasted too," wept Jig and Jog in dismay.

"Your cakes needn't be wasted!" said Dame Chippy. "I'll come in and eat them for you!"

And so she did – but Jig and Jog weren't a bit pleased. What sillies they were, weren't they?

# A lame duck and a stile

"I'm taking my doll for a walk, Mummy," said Amanda. "I've put her into her pram and tucked her up. We shall just go across the fields and back."

"You won't be able to take your pram over the stile," said Mummy, "so don't try."

"I won't," said Amanda. "I'll just walk as far as the stile, then I'll turn back. That will be a nice walk for Rosebud."

Rosebud was her doll, a small, lovely little thing, lying in the pram with her eyes shut. She aways shut them when she lay down. Mother said she wished babies would do that too. It would be so nice if they all went to sleep as soon as they were put down in prams or cots!

Rosebud opened her eyes when she sat up. She had blue eyes and golden hair. Amanda loved her very much. She liked taking her for walks in the pram. She often talked to her as she went along.

She talked to her that morning, although Rosebud was asleep, with her eyes shut.

"It's a lovely sunny day," said Amanda. "The buttercups are out all over the field, Rosebud. They are brushing against the wheels of the pram and making them all yellow."

Rosebud said nothing. She kept her eyes shut.

"The birds are singing," said Amanda. "I can hear them. Sit up and listen, Rosebud. It would do you good to be awake now."

She sat Rosebud up. Rosebud opened her blue eyes and looked at Amanda. She was a very smiley doll, and her smile showed two rows of tiny white teeth. Amanda sometimes tried to clean Rosebud's tiny teeth, but it wasn't easy.

"Now you can see the buttercups, and hear the birds singing," said Amanda. Then she stopped talking and looked puzzled.

"What's that noise?" she said. "It sounds like a very loud quacking!"

It was. "QUACK, QUACK, QUACK!" went the noise. "QUACK, QUACK, QUACK!"

"There aren't any ducks near here, surely?" said Amanda. "They all swim on the pond at the farm. Rosebud, we had better find out if it *is* a duck."

They went on down the path across the buttercup field. The noise grew louder. Amanda came to the stile and stopped.

The quacking seemed to come from the other side. She peeped over the stile. She was surprised to see a large white duck there, looking up at her out of bright eyes.

"Hallo!" said Amanda, rather startled. "What are you quacking for?"

"QUACK!" said the duck, and put its head through an opening under the stile.

"I see. You want to get over that stile," said Amanda. "Well, why don't you?"

"Quack, quack," said the duck, in a sad sort of voice.

Then Amanda saw that it had a bad foot. It had webbed skin between its toes to help it when it swam – but the webbing on one foot was torn. Now it was lame and could hardly get along on its one good foot.

"Poor thing! You can't get over the stile!" said Amanda, in pity. "I'll help you over. Mummy is always saying something about helping lame ducks over a stile, but I never thought *I* should do that! I thought it was just a saying that meant helping people in trouble."

But this time it was real. There was a real lame duck, trying to get over a

real stile, and Amanda was there to
help it.

She climbed over the stile, and tried
to push the duck through, over the
bottom bar. It was difficult because
the duck didn't seem to think that
Amanda was trying to help it. It gave
her a peck.

"Oh, don't do that when I'm trying
to help you!" said Amanda. "That's not
kind. Now – one more push – and over
you go, poor lame duck!"

This time the duck did go over the
stile and, much to its surprise, found
itself on the other side. This was where
it wanted to be.

It had swum out of the pond and down
the stream. Then it had caught its foot
on some sharp stones, and climbed on
to the bank because its foot hurt it too
much to swim. It thought it would go
home by the fields. But it hadn't been
able to get over the stile.

Now it was over. It looked up at
Amanda and said "Quack!" She thought

perhaps it meant "Thank you." It began to waddle slowly along the path, which led to the farm where its pond was. But it couldn't even waddle properly now. Its foot hurt it too much.

It sank down among the buttercups and gave a most doleful quack. Amanda looked at it in alarm.

"Can't you walk? You ought to get back to the farm and have your leg seen to. Try again."

The duck tried again, but once more it fell over. Amanda couldn't bear it. She wondered what to do.

"I know!" she said. "I'll wheel you in my pram. I once read a story about a little girl who wheeled a lost lamb home in her pram. So I don't see why I shouldn't wheel a lame duck."

She bent down to pick up the big, heavy duck. It pecked her hands.

"Don't!" said Amanda. "I'm only trying to help you! I can't leave you here. The fox might get you! He lives about these fields."

She bent down again, and again the duck pecked her and made a nasty sound in its throat. Amanda didn't know what to do. What an ungrateful duck!

She had one last try. She picked up the big duck and popped it into her pram! It pecked her again and tried to strike her with its wing. Amanda felt rather hurt.

"You're unkind," she said. "Oh, do keep still! You're sitting on poor Rosebud!"

The duck wriggled about in the pram, and then it pecked Rosebud's nose! Amanda was really cross.

"Now look here, Duck, I've done a lot for you, and I'm taking you home in Rosebud's pram. You've quacked at me and pecked me, and hit me with your wings – but you're *not* going to peck Rosebud! Sit still!"

After that the duck did sit still. It squatted comfortably down in the pram, leaving Rosebud just enough room, and quacked no more. It closed its eyes.

"Perhaps it likes being in the pram," thought Amanda, and wheeled it carefully along the path. She came to the farm and called to the farmer's wife.

"I've got one of your ducks in my pram. It has hurt its foot."

"Bless us all! Fancy wheeling it back here, you kind little thing!" cried Mrs Straw, and hurried to get the duck. It gave Amanda one last peck.

"It doesn't like me," said Amanda, almost in tears. "I only tried to help it. It keeps pecking me."

"Only because it is in pain, dear," said Mrs Straw, and took the duck away to see to its foot. "Thank you for bringing it home."

Amanda went home with Rosebud to tell her mother about the duck. "It wasn't a nice duck," she said. "It didn't like me, even when I tried to help it. It never even quacked a thank you."

Amanda was sad. She went to her pram to take Rosebud out – and then she got a surprise!

In the pram lay a big greenish-grey duck's egg! Amanda stared at it in the greatest astonishment. She picked it up and ran to her mother.

"Mummy! The duck's laid me an egg! It must have liked me after all! Look!"

"What a beauty!" said Mummy. "That's the best reward the duck could give you, isn't it? You can have it for your breakfast."

"But I don't like ducks' eggs," said Amanda. "I had one at Auntie's once and it tasted funny. I don't want to eat it, Mummy . . ."

"Well – shall we give it to Henny-Penny to sit on?" said Mummy. "She has ten of her own eggs to sit on, and she won't mind if we add this duck's egg to her batch. Then maybe you will have a little duckling of your own!"

Amanda thought that was a fine idea. She put the warm duck's egg with

Henny-Penny's big batch of brown eggs. Henny-Penny, the brown hen, didn't seem to mind a bit.

And do you know, out of that greenish-grey duck's egg came the dearest little yellow duckling you ever saw! Henny-Penny sat on her eggs for some weeks, and ten of them hatched into yellow chicks – and one into the duckling!

"It's *my* duckling!" cried Amanda, in delight. "My very own. You shall be my pet, little duckling. I shall call you Quack!"

I saw Quack yesterday, and Amanda told me this story. She thought you might like to hear it too.

"I helped a lame duck over a stile!" she said, "and that's how I got a duckling for my own. I *am* a lucky girl, aren't I?"

# *The ugly old toad*

Once upon a time a big old toad wanted to cross the road to get to a pond he knew on the other side. He couldn't jump high and quickly like his cousin the frog. He could only do small hops, or crawl, but he set off valiantly, hoping to get across the road before anything came along.

He was almost across when a horse and cart came down the lane. Clippitty-cloppitty, clippitty-cloppitty went the horse's hoofs, and the old toad heard them. He tried to hop away quickly, but one of the horse's hoofs trod on his back leg. Almost at once the horse lifted his hoof again and went on, not knowing that he had crushed the foot of the toad.

"Oh!" groaned the toad to himself, crawling to the side of the road, dragging his hurt foot behind him. "What a bit of bad luck! I can hardly walk now. How my foot is hurting me!"

He was in such pain that he could not go any farther. He squatted by the side of the road, hoping that his foot would soon get better. But it didn't.

He tried again to crawl, but his foot hurt him too much, so he lay there, half-hidden by a tuft of grass, hoping that no enemy would come by.

The big rat ran by and stopped when he saw the toad. "Aha! Dinner for me!" thought the rat, knowing that the toad was hurt. He ran up to the toad and snapped at him.

The toad still could not crawl away, but he had a good trick to play on the rat. He oozed out an evil-smelling, horrible-tasting liquid all over his back. When the rat tried to bite him, he got his mouth full of the nasty stuff.

"Horrible!" said the rat, and stood staring at the toad with his mouth open, trying to let the nasty-tasting stuff drip out of his mouth. "Horrible! I wouldn't have *you* for my dinner for anything!"

He ran off, and the toad sat still, glad to be rid of him. Then he heard footsteps coming down the lane, and he shrank back into the grass, trying to look like a brown clod of earth. He really did look like one.

Soon a boy came up, whistling. He almost trod on the toad, but he did not see him and went whistling on. He thought the old toad was just a lump of earth.

He stayed still, hoping that his foot would stop hurting. But the horse's hoof had been hard and heavy – it was a wonder it had not cut the toad's foot right off.

Then the toad heard more footsteps – lighter ones this time. He crouched down again, but this time the passer-by was sharper-eyed than the boy.

"Ooh! A toad!" said a voice, and the toad, looking up cautiously, saw a little girl gazing down at him. She wrinkled her nose in disgust.

"Nasty creature! I can't bear toads! Ugly thing with your pimply back and your creepy-crawly ways! I don't like you a bit!"

The toad crouched very still. He was afraid. This little girl might stamp on him – children were sometimes very cruel to creatures like him. But he couldn't help being an ugly old toad – he was born like that.

However, the little girl did not stamp on him. She wasn't cruel. She did think the toad was ugly, and she didn't like him much, but she wasn't going to be unkind.

"I don't like ugly creatures," she said to the toad. "I couldn't bear to touch you. Oooh, that *would* be horrid! It would make me feel ill."

The toad was sad. He wished he had been born a butterfly or a bird. Then perhaps the little girl would have liked him. But you had to be what you were born to be – there wasn't any help for it.

Then suddenly the little girl saw the toad's foot. It was all crushed and flattened. She stared at it in horror.

"Toad! Your foot is squashed to bits! Is it hurting you? Oh, how did that happen? Did someone tread on you?"

The toad still crouched flat. He knew the little girl wouldn't tread on him now, but he was still afraid. She looked at him, sad because of his foot.

"Oh, I can't leave you here like this," she said. "I'm sorry I said all those unkind things now. I didn't know you were hurt. I think I had better take you home to my mother – she will know what to do with your foot."

The toad didn't want to be taken home. He wanted to be left alone in peace. The little girl was wondering how to carry him.

"Although I am very sorry for you, I simply *can't* touch you," she said. "I can't! I should drop you if I touched you. You see, I don't like toads."

Then she thought of using her handkerchief. She would wrap the toad in that and carry him by taking hold of the four corners of the hanky. Then she would not need to touch him at all.

So to the toad's surprise and fright, she dropped her hanky over him, rolled him gently into it, and picked him up in the hanky. She carried him by taking hold of the four corners, but she didn't even like doing that!

She took him home. The toad did not wriggle or struggle, because it hurt his foot too much. He just lay in the hanky, very miserable, wondering what was going to happen to him.

The little girl went in at her gate. She called to her mother. "Mummy! I've got a hurt toad. Can you do something for him?"

Her mother was very surprised. She undid the hanky and took the toad in her bare hands. She didn't mind touching any creature. She saw the hurt foot and was sorry.

"I can't do much," she said. "I will just bathe it with very weak iodine – but it's no good binding it up. The best thing you can do for him, Jenny, is to put him in a cool, shady corner of the garden, where there are plenty of flies for him to catch, and leave him to himself. Maybe the foot will heal itself."

"I don't like him much," said Jenny.

"He can't help being a toad," said her mother. "*You* might have been born a toad – and think how sad you would be if people hated you, and tried to hurt you because you happened to be ugly. That's not fair, Jenny."

"No, it isn't," said Jenny. She looked down at the toad, and he looked up at her. She saw his eyes.

"Mummy, he's got the most beautiful eyes!" she said, surprised. "Do look at them. They are like jewels in his head, gleaming as bright as copper."

"All toads have lovely eyes," said

Mummy. "They are nice creatures, Jenny, and make good pets."

"Oh, *no*, Mummy!" said Jenny, astonished. "I have never heard of a toad as a pet before!"

"There are quite a lot of things you haven't heard of!" said Mummy. "Now – I've finished bathing his foot – do you think you can possibly bring yourself to carry him in your hands to a nice bit of the garden – or do you dislike toads so much?"

Jenny felt a bit ashamed of herself. She looked down at the toad. His coppery eyes gleamed kindly at her. He looked patient and wise.

"I'll carry him," she said, and she picked him up gently in her hands. He kept quite still. Jenny took him down the garden and put him in the cool hedge behind Daddy's lettuces.

"There you are!" she said. "Stay there and catch flies. I don't know what else you eat, but there are heaps of flies here for you."

There were. The toad heard a big one buzzing just over his head. He looked at it – and then, quick as a flash, he shot out a long sticky tongue, caught the fly on the tip of it, swallowed, and looked at Jenny.

"A good meal," he seemed to say. Jenny laughed.

"You're rather nice," she said, and left him.

She forgot all about him. A week went by, then two weeks. Then Daddy came in one evening, bringing two delicious lettuces for supper.

"Good gracious!" said Mummy, pleased. "I thought you told me that all your lettuces had been eaten by slugs, Daddy. What beauties these are!"

"Ah! I've got someone to guard my lettuces for me!" said Daddy. "And a very good fellow he is, too. He never allows a single slug on my lettuce-bed now."

"Who is he?" said Jenny, puzzled.

"He's a toad," said Daddy, "a wise,

friendly, kind old toad. He lives in the hedge behind my kitchen garden, and he keeps guard over the lettuces. See how well they have grown since the old toad looked after them for me!"

"Daddy! He must be *my* toad! I forgot all about him," said Jenny, excited.

"*Your* toad? I thought you didn't like toads," said Daddy. "What do you mean?"

Jenny told him. "And we shall know if it *is* my toad by his foot," she said. "Has he got a mended foot, Daddy?"

"I didn't notice," said Daddy. "Let's go and see."

So they went to see – and there was the old toad, and behind him was his hurt foot – mended and healed now, but rather a funny shape.

"It *is* my toad!" said Jenny. "Look, he's crawling over to me, Daddy. He knows I'm the little girl who brought him home."

"Tickle his back with a grass," said Daddy. "He'll like that."

So Jenny did, and the toad liked it very much. He tried to scratch his back with one of his feet, and made Jenny laugh.

"You're a good old toad," she said. "I like you, and you shall be my pet."

He *is* her pet, and he still keeps guard over the kitchen garden. I know because I've seen him there!

## *The poor little owl*

In the field nearby lived a little brown owl. John and Betty often saw it sitting on the telegraph wires in the dusk, when they went to bed.

"Tvit, tvit, tvit!" said the little owl to them, and the children called "Tvit, tvit!" back to it. It wasn't very big, and when it spread its wings it flew very silently indeed.

Then one evening, as John and Betty walked home, they saw the little owl disappear into a hole in an old, old willow tree.

"I guess it has got its nest there!" said John in excitement. "I wonder if there will be any baby owls. We must watch and see."

But before they knew, a sad thing happened to the little owl. It went to drink from the pond one night, overbalanced, fell into the water and couldn't get out! So in the morning John and Betty found that it was drowned, and they were very sad.

"Oh, John – what about the baby owls, if there are any in the tree?" said Betty in tears. "There won't be anyone to feed them. They will starve to death, poor things."

John spoke to the gardener about the nest he was sure was in the old willow tree. "Couldn't you look and see if there are any baby owls there?" he said. "We don't want them to starve, you know."

"I'm not going after any owls," said the gardener at once. "Dangerous creatures they are, with their sharp claws! My goodness, even a baby owl can get its claws into you so hard that you can't get them out."

"Oh," said John. He went away, but he kept on and on thinking about the owls. He felt sure they were hungry and unhappy.

"Betty, there must be *some* way of getting them out," he said. "Do think. You're clever at thinking."

So Betty thought. "Well," she said, "if their claws are so sharp and strong that they can dig right into your hand and not let it go, what about letting down something into the nest — a handkerchief, perhaps — and letting them dig their claws into that. Then all we need to do is to draw up the handkerchief and the owls will come too!"

"Marvellous idea!" cried John. And so it was. Betty borrowed a big old silk hanky from Daddy's drawer, and the two children went to the old willow tree. They climbed up it and came to the hole, which went deep into a thick branch of the tree.

A faint hissing noise came up from the hole. "Goodness – is there a snake in there?" said Betty.

"No! Owls do hiss, you know," said John. "Now, Betty – where's the hanky? Hand it over."

John took the hanky and let one end slowly down into the hole. There were two baby owls in the tree. They turned themselves over so that their clawed feet were on top – and how they attacked that silk hanky! They dug their feet into it and their claws caught in the silk.

"Got them nicely!" shouted John, and

he pulled up the hanky. There were the two fluffy baby owls holding on to it for all they were worth! John popped them into a box he had brought with him, shut the lid, and then switched his torch on to see the nest.

"There isn't really any nest," he called to Betty, "just a few shavings from the hole, that's all. But wait a minute – what's this?"

The light of his torch had shone on to something red. John put his hand into the hole and felt what it was. It seemed to be a little bag of some sort. He pulled at it – and it came out. It was heavy.

"Betty! The owl had made her nest on top of this little bag!" cried John. "Look – it's got the name of the bank on it. I do believe it's the bag of gold that a thief stole from the bank messenger last winter! He must have hidden it here and then forgotten where the hiding place was!"

"Goodness!" said Betty, as John

opened the little red bag and a whole heap of shining golden coins winked up at them. "What a lot of money! Come and tell Mummy."

Well, that was a most exciting afternoon. The children had two baby owls for pets, and a bag of gold to give back to the bank! And what do you think? The bank manager gave the children one of the pieces of gold!

"That's your reward," he said. "Buy what you like with it."

So what do you think they bought with the money? They went to the shops and bought a marvellous cage in which to bring up their two pet owls! It was painted blue outside, and had red perches inside, and was very grand and big indeed.

"You can keep your little owls there and bring them up in safety till they are big enough to fly away and look after themselves," said their mother. "You must feed them well, give them fresh water, and clean out their cage every single day."

So they did, and soon the two owls grew tame and friendly, and sat peacefully on the children's fingers whenever they were held out to them. Betty and John were very proud of their pets, because no one else at school had owls; and even the teacher came to see them, and said what strange and curious birds they were.

"They look rather like little feathered cats!" she said. And so they did, as they sat side by side on their perches, their big golden eyes looking solemnly at the visitor.

And now they have flown away to look after themselves; but John and Betty have left the cage door open in case they might like to come back there to sleep. I expect they will sometimes.

Every night the two little birds call to their friends and say "Tvit, tvit, tvit!" from the nearby field. I wonder if *you* have heard them. They call so sharply and so loudly that I shouldn't be a bit surprised if you hear them too!

## *The little girl who cried*

"Anna's always got red eyes," said Lucy. "She's a baby. She's always crying."

"Cry-baby, cry-baby!" said Katie, pointing her finger at Anna, who was coming along wiping her eyes. She had just fallen down and hurt her knee.

That made Anna begin to cry all over again. She really was a cry-baby, but she hated being called one.

Poor Anna! She cried if she fell down. She cried if her porridge was too hot. She cried if she made a mistake in her writing book. She cried if she thought she was going to be late for school, and she cried if anyone scolded her.

"For goodness sake, Anna, don't turn

on the tap again!" said Lucy. "Where do you get all your tears from? I never knew anyone cry such buckets of tears. You should do very, very well as a watering-can."

Everybody laughed except Anna. She wept a few more tears. "You're unkind," she said. "You *make* me cry. I'm very unhappy."

"You're a little silly," said Katie. "You just *let* yourself cry! *We* could cry, too, when we fall down and hurt ourselves – but we don't. We just press our lips together hard and get up and rub our knees and go on playing. We won't *let* ourselves cry."

The children teased poor Anna a good deal. It really was quite a joke with them to make Anna cry. It was so easy!

"If anyone jumps out and says 'BOO!' Anna cries," said Lucy. "And if you say 'Silly-Billy' she cries. And if you take away her pencil she cries. Let's tease her and get her out of the habit of crying. It's the only way."

But it wasn't a good way with Anna. She grew frightened of the others, and began to hate going to school. She seemed to cry all day long and her teacher was worried about her.

So one day she asked Anna to tea, and Anna went. There were crumpets for tea, well toasted, and a homemade chocolate cake, and homemade strawberry jam. So Anna enjoyed herself and for a whole hour not a single tear came into her eyes.

After tea Miss Brown pulled two chairs up to the fire and began to talk.

"You know, Anna," she said, "I really am pleased that you haven't cried yet. You look so nice when you are smiling, and your eyes are bright and merry, instead of being full of tears and sad."

Anna looked at herself in the mirror. Yes, she certainly did look nicer. But even as she thought of how the others teased her and made her cry, the tears came into her eyes!

"Well, if you haven't begun again!" said Miss Brown, laughing. "What shall we do with you? I believe you *like* crying, Anna."

"Oh, I don't, I don't," said Anna at once. "I'm ashamed of it, I really am. I hate being a cry-baby. But I suppose I always shall be."

"You certainly will if you think like that," said Miss Brown. "We make ourselves what we are, you know."

"But I don't know how to stop," said poor Anna. "Oh, how I wish I was someone brave and great and fearless, not myself."

"I know what you could do!" said Miss Brown. "You could pretend to be Anna the Fearless!"

"Who was she?" said Anna in surprise. "I've never heard of her."

"She was a very brave peasant-girl in a far-off country," said Miss Brown. "Enemies came to look for her father and brothers, who were hiding in a wood nearby. They found Anna and tried to make her say where they were."

"And did she?" said Anna.

"No," said Miss Brown. "So the enemy thought they would treat her cruelly, make her cry bitterly, and then perhaps she would give her people away. So they beat her, but Anna didn't cry a single tear."

"She was brave," said Anna.

"She was proud," said Miss Brown, "too proud to weep. She did not mean to show her enemies that they hurt her. So she stood there, her mouth tight shut, her face white, but she did not let a single tear trickle down her cheek in case the enemy thought she was weakening. Then they burnt down her house, but even when she saw the flames Anna would not give away her father and brothers, nor beg for mercy, nor cry."

"Oh, Miss Brown – she *must* have been brave!" said Anna, her eyes shining. "What happened then?"

"The enemy said they were sure the little girl did not know where her father and brothers were, or she would certainly have told them, or cried bitterly," said Miss Brown. "So they left her there and went away. And her father and brothers came out of their hiding-place, and hugged her and praised her for her fearlessness and loyalty."

"I wish I was that Anna," said Anna. "Oh, how I wish I was as brave as that."

"Do you really?" said Miss Brown. "Well, listen, Anna. You can never be *that* little Anna because you are yourself and always will be. But why don't you *pretend* to be that other Anna, when people tease you, or you fall down and hurt yourself, or things go wrong? Say to yourself then, 'I am Anna the Fearless and I will not cry!' I don't believe you will be able to weep a single tear if you do that."

"Oh, Miss Brown, I'll try it!" said Anna in delight. "I really will. If I *pretend* to be brave, that's the next best thing to *being* brave, isn't it?"

"It's very often the same thing!" said Miss Brown. "Now go home and think about it. I hope by the end of the term that I really shall have a little Anna the Fearless in my class."

Anna felt excited. She went home. She thought about it. She went to bed and dreamed about it. She *would* be like Anna the Fearless, she would!

She set off to school, and met Lucy and Katie. "Hallo, here's the silly cry-baby!" said Lucy. "Pull her hair!"

They pulled Anna's hair, but she

pursed up her lips and pulled her head away from them. "I'm Anna the Fearless!" she thought to herself. "What do I care for enemies? What do I care about bad names and pulled hair? Nothing at all. I'm Anna the Fearless."

So, to the great surprise of the others, not a tear rolled down Anna's cheek. They all went on to school talking. Just as they got to the school-gate Harry came along and pushed Anna roughly

against the gate-post. She grazed her arm, and tears sprang to her eyes. But at once she spoke to herself proudly.

"I'm Anna the Fearless! What do I care about a silly grazed arm? Nothing at all. My enemies shall never make me cry!"

So she blinked back the tears and not one rolled down her cheek. Harry was surprised.

"No tears this morning?" he said. "What's happened to our cry-baby?"

The bell rang and the children ran to take their places. School began, and lesson after lesson was taken.

In writing-lesson John jogged Anna's arm, and her pen shot across the page and spoilt her work. Usually Anna would have wailed aloud, cried bitterly, and told tales. But today she glared at John, pursed up her lips, and said nothing. John waited to see the tears come, but none came. Anna the Fearless was not going to cry over a little thing like that.

At playtime the children rushed out, laughing and shouting. They played catch in the garden, and had a fine time. The day was rather wet, and the ground was muddy. As she ran, Anna slipped and fell. She hurt both her knees and one hand. She got up at once, and the others crowded round her, expecting to see floods of tears, and to hear loud yells.

"Bother," said Anna in a loud, clear voice. "Now my knees are bleeding, and I'll have to wash them."

"One's quite bad, Anna," said Lucy, feeling sorry. "Poor old Anna. Never mind."

The kind words almost made Anna cry. But she held up her head proudly. "I'm Anna the Fearless," she thought. "I don't cry about hurt knees and hands. Nobody can make me cry if I don't want to. My enemies shall never see me cry. I'm brave and fearless, and I've more courage than all the others put together."

Her knees hurt her and her hand bled. But she even managed a funny little smile when Miss Brown bathed the bruises and bandaged her knees.

"You're Anna the Fearless, aren't you?" whispered Miss Brown. "I thought you were. Anna, you are marvellous. Keep it up, won't you?"

"It's fun to pretend I am what I'm not when it's something so much grander and better than myself," said Anna. "I know I'm a baby, and silly and weak, but I feel fine when I'm pretending to be brave and grand."

Miss Brown smiled a secret little smile. "You will find it isn't all pretence, if you keep it up long enough," she said.

"I'll keep it up till the end of the term, then I think I'll have a rest, and be myself in the holidays," said Anna. "It's really not very easy, you know, Miss Brown, although it's fun. I'll go back to being silly again in the holidays, but in school I'll always be Anna the Fearless now."

So she went on being Anna the Fearless for the rest of the term, and soon the children gave up teasing her, because it wasn't any fun. Anna didn't cry any more. She was braver than the biggest child. She didn't seem to care when she was hurt or teased. The children thought she was quite different and very much nicer.

"And now, Anna, I suppose you won't be Anna the Fearless after today," said Miss Brown at the end of the term. "You'll be the poor little frightened Anna I knew at the beginning of the term."

"I expect so," said Anna. "I've tried very hard, Miss Brown, and now I want a rest. I shan't be Anna the Fearless in the holidays."

But wasn't it an extraordinary thing? Anna couldn't stop being Anna the Fearless! She had pretended to be brave and courageous so long that now she really was. She couldn't cry at little things. It was natural for her to be brave now. She could never, never be cry-baby Anna again.

"Well, what a funny thing," said Anna, and she ran to tell Miss Brown after three days of the holidays. Miss Brown smiled.

"I rather thought this would happen," she said, giving Anna a hug. "I told you we make our own selves what we are, didn't I? Brave or cowardly, kind or selfish, good or bad. Well, you made yourself different by acting like somebody else. You really are a little Anna the Fearless now, and always will be. I'm proud of you, Anna; really proud of you. You need never be afraid of being a cry-baby again."

I know Anna very well, and she is one of the finest, bravest children I know; but she certainly wasn't always like that. It's a very good idea of Miss Brown's, isn't it – to pretend to be someone braver, or kinder or stronger than yourself? Because, you always end up really being like that!

## Brer Rabbit plays a trick

Once Brer Rabbit had a fine crop of pickling onions, and he stood and looked at them, wondering what to do with so many.

"I've pickled all I want for myself," he said to Brer Terrapin, "and you don't like onions. What am I to do with so many, Brer Terrapin?"

"Pickle them in big jars and sell them to Mr Benjamin Ram!" said Brer Terrapin. "He's fond of onions, he is. He'll pay you a good price for them, Brer Rabbit. You get some good big jars and pickle the biggest onions you've got!"

So Brer Rabbit got some enormous stone jars and filled them full of onions in vinegar – my, how good they smelt!

Brer Terrapin sniffed them and wished he liked them. "Now, you ask old Benjamin Ram to dinner," he said, "and let him taste those. If he doesn't buy the whole lot from you I'll eat my shell!"

Mr Benjamin Ram came to dinner, and brought his violin. *Plink, plonk, plonk!* it went, as Brer Rabbit set out the dinner. Then Mr Benjamin Ram stopped his playing and sniffed.

"What's that nice smell?" he said.

"My pickled onions," said Brer Rabbit. "I know you're fond of them, Benjamin Ram."

He certainly was! He ate twenty-one, and Brer Rabbit marvelled at him.

Then he pushed back his chair, wiped his long beard, and said, "Best I've ever tasted. Ask me to dinner again, Brer Rabbit."

"I've got plenty of pickled onions to sell," said Brer Rabbit. "Cheap, too."

"Then I'll buy them – the whole lot!" said Mr Benjamin Ram. "Here you are

– here's my purse. Empty it, and let me have all the jars of onions you've got."

There was a lot of money in Mr Ram's purse. Brer Rabbit emptied it into his own pocket, very pleased. Then he got down the big jars of pickled onions from the shelves in his cupboard.

"There you are," he said. "Eight fine jars – enough to last you a month, Benjamin Ram. Shall I put them into a sack for you?"

"No," said Benjamin Ram. "I'm going to visit my old aunt, Bessie Ram – and she's fonder of pickled onions than I am. She would eat the lot. You deliver them for me, Brer Rabbit. I've paid you enough money for that, too."

He said goodnight and went, playing his violin all the way through the wood. Brer Rabbit could hear it – *plink, plonk, plunk, plink, plonk, plunk!*

He looked at the eight big jars. How was he going to carry all those? They were very, very heavy.

"If I carry them all at once, I'll never get there," thought Brer Rabbit. "And if I take them one at a time it would mean eight long journeys there and back."

He sat and thought hard. He saw someone passing his front gate – it was old Brer Bear carrying a sack of potatoes back home. It was a big heavy sack, but Brer Bear didn't mind. He was stronger than anyone else in the wood.

Brer Rabbit stared after him, and an idea began to bubble in his mind. Yes, *he* knew how to get those jars of pickled onions to Mr Benjamin Ram! Aha – it would be easy.

Brer Bear lived quite near Mr Benjamin Ram. Why shouldn't *he* carry a large sack full of jars of pickled onions all the way to Benjamin's house – and save Brer Rabbit's poor old back?

But it wouldn't be any good *asking* Brer Bear to do that. He was a surly fellow, and he wasn't at all fond of wily Brer Rabbit. No, Brer Rabbit would have to make him carry them by some clever little trick!

But what trick could it be?

Brer Rabbit sat with his head in his hands and his ears down, thinking hard again. And then his furry ears rose up straight and Brer Rabbit laughed out loud. "Of course! *I* know how to make Brer Bear carry my jars of pickled onions for me! Look out now, Brer Bear, you're going to have a heavy load soon!"

Well, what did Brer Rabbit do but take off all the labels on his jars that said PICKLED ONIONS and put another set on instead. On these he printed one word in very big letters indeed: HONEY.

He looked at the jars and chuckled. They were labelled HONEY – but they were full of onions. Brer Bear didn't like onions – but he *loved* honey.

"There's a nice little trick going to be played on you, Brer Bear," chuckled Brer Rabbit, as he went off to fetch a sack.

He put all the jars into the sack, and then went to bed. Next morning he took the heavy sack, full of the jars, and carried it, puffing and panting, into the wood. He set the sack down near the path, half under a bush. It was the path that Brer Bear used every day!

Then he hid himself under another bush and waited for Brer Bear to come lumbering by.

Soon he heard the tattling Jack Sparrow up in the tree calling out loudly. "Here comes Brer Bear, have a care, have a care, here comes Brer Bear, beware, beware!"

Brer Bear came along, sniffing here and there as he went, his little eyes looking into every corner. He suddenly saw the sack half hidden under a bush, and went quickly over to it.

"What's this?" said Brer Bear, and he opened the sack and looked inside. At once he saw the jars, each one labelled HONEY.

"Honey! Jars of honey – big ones, too!" said Brer Bear, amazed. "I've not tasted honey for a week. Who does all this belong to?"

He called, "Anyone about?"

But nobody answered.

Brer Bear peered here and peered there, and then he picked up the sack. It was heavy but he was so strong that it felt as light as a feather to him. He put it carefully over his shoulder and set off.

"Well, if there's nobody to look after a sack of honey jars, I don't mind taking on the job myself," he said. "My, what a feast I'll have!"

Brer Rabbit watched him carrying away the sack and laughed. You wait, Brer Bear, you'll get a shock in a minute!

Brer Rabbit scampered through the wood and got right in front of Brer Bear. He ran till he came to Mr Benjamin Ram's house. Benjamin was out in his garden, smoking his pipe and digging hard.

"Mr Benjamin Ram, I've bad news for you," panted Brer Rabbit. "I put your pickled onion jars into a sack and carried it as far as the path through the wood – and I put it down for a minute under a bush – and will you believe it, someone came along and took it. It's gone."

"What? My pickled onions!" said Mr Ram, in a rage. "What next? I've paid for them, haven't I? They're mine, aren't they? How *dare* someone come along and take my sack of pickled onions. Who was it?"

"It was old Brer Bear," said Brer Rabbit, grinning. "He lives near you, doesn't he, Mr Ram? Well, you'll see him passing by in a little while and you can stop him and get them from him. I'll wait here and see fair play."

Mr Benjamin Ram was really very angry – so angry that he longed to rush at somebody and butt him hard! He waited and waited for Brer Bear to come by.

Brer Bear came in sight, the sack over his shoulder.

Mr Benjamin Ram rushed out at once, shouting, "Hey, Brer Bear, you've got my pickled onions. You drop them at once, or I'll butt you."

Brer Bear stared at Mr Ram in amazement. "*I* haven't got your onions!" he said. "I don't know what you're talking about. I've got jars of honey in here."

"I don't believe you," said Mr Ram. "Let me see, or I'll butt you."

He looked so very fierce that Brer Bear hurriedly put down the sack and undid it. Mr Ram peered inside and saw the stone jars, all labelled HONEY.

"There you are, Mr Ram," said Brer Bear. "What did I tell you? Honey!"

"Ah – that's what the *label* says!" said Brer Rabbit, sauntering up, twiddling his whiskers. "But what's *inside* the jars?"

"Honey, of course," said Brer Bear, and then he began to tell a lot of stories.

"I went to market this very morning, so I did. And I bought these eight jars of best honey. They were a fine price, too. There are no onions in these jars, it's just best honey – and what's more I'm taking it home to my old missus, this very minute."

"Well, if you bought the jars at the market full of honey, you won't mind if we look inside one, will you?" said Brer Rabbit. "Then you can laugh at us for thinking they were full of onions!" And with that he unscrewed a lid – and out came a very strong smell of pickled onions!

Brer Bear was full of astonishment. He stared at the onions as if he couldn't believe his eyes. Onions! In jars labelled HONEY. He couldn't understand it at all!

"My onions!" shouted Mr Benjamin Ram and ran straight at the surprised Brer Bear.

He butted him so hard that Brer Bear rose in the air and flew over a bush –

and landed with a thump on the other side. He got up and lumbered away as fast as he could go, very puzzled indeed.

"Well – you've got your onions," said Brer Rabbit.

"Why did you label them HONEY?" asked Mr Benjamin Ram, putting the sack over his back to take them to his house. "Seems funny to me, Brer Rabbit."

"Oh, you work it out," said Brer Rabbit, and away he skipped through the trees to catch up with poor Brer Bear.

Brer Bear was on his way home, still puzzled, rubbing a very big bruise where Mr Benjamin Ram had butted him. He wasn't at all pleased to see Brer Rabbit.

"Heyo, Brer Bear!" said Brer Rabbit. "Thanks for carrying that heavy sack to Mr Ram's for me."

"What do you mean, Brer Rabbit?" asked Brer Bear, fiercely.

"Well, it was too heavy for *me*," said
Brer Rabbit. "So I left it for you to pick
up. I just labelled the jars HONEY."

And with that he skipped out of
Brer Bear's way, and then rolled on
the ground and laughed till the tears
dripped off his nose.

Poor Brer Bear – he's no match for old
Brer Rabbit!

# A pins and needles spell

"We're going to have a meeting this afternoon to decide what to give Princess Peronel for a birthday present," said Whiskers, the brownie, to Jinks and Cheery.

"Well, don't ask old Meanie then," said Jinks. "He made an awful fuss last year, and wouldn't vote even a penny towards a present."

"And the little Princess is *such* a dear," said Cheery. "Always a smile and a wave for everyone. I vote we buy her a pair of dancing shoes for her nimble little feet, and get the Pixie Fly-High to fetch a couple of tiny stars from the sky, to put on the slippers' toes. Think how her feet would twinkle when she dances!"

"Now that's a really bright idea!" said Whiskers, pleased. "Bring it up at the meeting, Cheery. It's to be held in the Toadstool Wood, and Gobo is growing a few toadstools for us to sit on."

"Right. I'll tell the others," said Jinks. "But we *won't* ask old Meanie!"

They didn't ask Meanie – but he heard of the meeting, of course, and was very angry because he hadn't been invited. He went straight to Gobo, Jinks and Cheery.

"I shall come!" he said, "and what's more I shall talk the whole time, and tell you what nonsense it is to give presents to a rich Princess, and nobody else will get a word in!"

"You did that last time," said Gobo. "That's why we're not asking you to the meeting. You can't come if you're not asked."

"That's just where you're wrong!" said Meanie, fiercely. "I *shall* come.

I know where you're all meeting – in the Toadstool Wood!"

"I forbid you to come!" said Gobo, sternly. "And don't you dare to disobey – or I'll put a dreadful spell on you!"

"Don't be so silly," said Meanie. "*You* put a spell on *me*? Why, you couldn't put a spell on a beetle! What *sort* of spell, I'd like to know?"

"I might put a tick-tock spell on you," said Gobo. "So that you could only tick-tock like a clock, instead of speaking. Or a sleepy spell, so that you fell asleep. Or a pins and needles spell . . ."

"And what exactly is *that*?" said Meanie, mockingly. "I've never heard of it in my life – and neither have you, Gobo. This is all a bit of make-believe! Pins and needles spell, indeed!"

"A pins and needles spell is a spell that, quite suddenly, makes you feel as if there are pins and needles sticking into you!" said Gobo, solemnly. "It's very, very uncomfortable. I think I

*will* put that spell on you, Meanie —
and when *that* works, I'll put *another*
one on you — the tick-tock one, that
will make everyone laugh at you!"

And, to the surprise of Jinks and
Cheery, Gobo suddenly clapped his
hands and danced all round the
surprised Meanie, singing loudly.

"Here's a pins and needles spell,
Prick him, *jab him*,
Make him yell,
Here's a pins and needles SPELL!"

Meanie laughed. "Well? Where are
your pins and needles? *I* haven't felt
any! Don't try and make spells, Gobo
— you don't know anything about
them."

"Oh, the spell will only work if you
come and spoil our meeting," said Gobo,
solemnly. "Not unless. So keep away,
Meanie, unless you want suddenly to
feel jabbed and pricked all over!"

Meanie went off, still laughing. "I'll
come to the meeting all right," he

shouted back. "And I'll certainly tell you what I think about spending our money on Princesses!"

"Horrid fellow!" said Cheery. "Why, our little Princess Peronel is our great friend – we've watched her grow up from a tiny baby into the merriest child in the kingdom. Gobo, you shouldn't have said that spell – you *know* it won't work! You don't know any magic, and never have. You'll only make us look foolish this afternoon, when Meanie comes to the meeting, and no spell happens!"

"You wait and see," said Gobo. "There are more ways than one of making a spell happen. I can do spells without magic!"

"Rubbish!" said Jinks. "Well – we'll see you at the meeting. You've got to grow fifteen toadstools – sixteen, if Meanie comes, and I'm pretty certain he will."

That afternoon Gobo was very busy. He grew toadstool after toadstool for seats. He draped each one with little cloths that hung to the ground, for Gobo liked to do things well.

Then he disappeared into the ditch, and talked to someone there for a long time. Who was it? Ah, you wait and see! Anyway, the someone came to the ring of toadstools with him, and stood there patiently while Gobo draped *him* with a little cloth, too! He looked exactly like another seat.

The brownies began to come to the meeting in twos and threes. Gobo showed them to their seats. "No — don't sit *there*," he kept saying, pointing to one draped seat. "That's for Meanie, if he comes. It's a seat with a *pins and needles spell!*"

"Dear old Gobo — *you* can't make spells — you know you can't!" said Cheery. "Now, just don't say any more about pins and needles, for goodness sake."

Soon they were all sitting down, and the draped toadstool seats each held a brownie. Only one seat had no one on it – and that was the empty one left for Meanie – if he came.

The meeting began – and no Meanie was there. Cheery got up and made a splendid little speech about birthdays, and how they gave everyone a good chance to show people how much you loved them. So what kind of a present should they give Peronel?

And then a loud laugh came through the trees, and Meanie strode into the toadstool ring. "I heard your silly speech!" he cried. "A lot of nonsense. Now just let me tell you what *I* think!"

"Sit down," said Cheery. "It's Jinks's turn to speak next. SIT DOWN, I SAY!"

"Here's *your* seat, Meanie," said Gobo, and pointed to the empty one. Meanie glared round and sat down in a temper – sat down very hard indeed.

Then he suddenly gave such a loud yell that the brownie next to him fell

right off his toadstool in fright.

"Oooooh!" bellowed Meanie, "the pins and needles spell! Ooooh!"

And he leapt up into the air as if he had been stung and ran wailing through the trees, clutching the back of his trousers as he went.

"Good gracious – what's the matter with *him*?" said Whiskers, in surprise.

"Pins and needles. Ooooooh!" came Meanie's voice in the distance.

"What does he mean?" said Jinks, in wonder. "Goodness me – you don't mean to say your spell *worked*, Gobo?"

"It seems to have worked very well," said Gobo, grinning. "Anyway – now Meanie's gone – let's get on with the meeting."

They all sat down again, and then Jinks got up to make *his* speech. "I am happy to think that now Meanie has been sent away by Gobo's extraordinary pins and needles spell we can get on with our meeting," he began. Then he stopped suddenly and stared in fright at the one empty seat – the seat that had been Meanie's!

"I say – look! Meanie's seat is walking off!" cried Jinks, in a panic. "*Walking*! Whoever heard of a toadstool *walking*? I'm scared! What with pins and needles spells and walking toadstools . . ."

Gobo began to laugh. He laughed and he laughed. Then he beamed round at everyone. "Didn't I tell you there was more than one way of making spells happen? Well, let me show you how *mine* happened!" And he began to run after the draped seat that was solemnly walking away all by itself. "Hey, pins and needles, stop!"

The seat stopped. Gobo ran up to it and tore off the cloth that was round it.

And will you believe it – it was a prickly *hedgehog*!

The hedgehog promptly curled itself up into a spiky ball, and Gobo laughed. "There you are!" he said to his friends. "My pins and needles spell . . . the hedgehog! I just got him to come here and let me drape a covering over him. Wasn't he a *wonderful* spell? I never *dreamed* that Meanie would sit down quite so hard!"

How everyone roared! Whiskers held his sides and laughed so much that he had to lie down and roll on the grass.

"A pins and needles spell — and it was only Prickles the hedgehog! Oh, to think you've got rid of that awful Meanie by playing a silly trick on him like that!"

"And Meanie *sat* on Prickles — sat down hard in a temper!" cried Cheery. "Oh, I shall never forget this, all my life long. Gobo, you may be no good at *real* spells — but you are *wonderful* at pretend ones!"

Gobo couldn't help feeling pleased. "Now perhaps you won't laugh at me quite so much because I know so little magic," he said. "Well — let's get on with the meeting!"

So there they are, deciding to buy those dancing slippers for Princess Peronel, and wondering who can get the stars to twinkle on the toes — and laughing out loud whenever they think of poor well-pricked Meanie. He'll never come back again, that's certain. He's *much* too scared of clever old Gobo!

## The impatient wizard

Once upon a time there was a most impatient wizard. His name was Mr Shout and it was a good one, because whenever he felt impatient he shouted at the top of his voice.

His servant was a scared little brownie called Oh-Dear-Me, with a long beard that was always tripping him up. He was frightened of Mr Shout, and would have left him long ago if it hadn't been for the wizard's dog, Thunder.

Thunder had a growl so exactly like a roll of thunder that there really was no better name for him. He could *look* as black as thunder too and Oh-Dear-Me, the brownie, was even more scared of him than he was of Mr Shout. But he knew that if he ran away Thunder would most certainly catch him.

"Where are you, Oh-Dear-Me!" shouted the wizard from morning to night. "Fetch me a mushroom grown in the light of the moon. I want to make a spell. And bring me a glass of morning dew. And find a spider's web and some caterpillar hairs. I am doing much magic today!"

So it went on, and little Oh-Dear-Me ran about, panting, trying to keep out of the way of Thunder the dog and bring back everything that Mr Shout wanted. He tripped over his beard so often that Mr Shout threatened to cut it off.

"Oh dear me, don't do that!" begged the brownie, in alarm. "I wouldn't be a brownie if I had no beard. Oh dear me, what a terrible job I've got. Get away, Thunder – don't breathe down my neck like that. I haven't had time to make your bone for you yet."

Mr Shout didn't *buy* bones for Thunder. He had given little Oh-Dear-Me a spell for making a large bone each day. It was a very curious spell, and Oh-Dear-Me was a little bit afraid of it.

He made it each day at tea-time while Thunder the dog sat nearby, growling and watching. Oh-Dear-Me was sure that if he ever made a mistake Thunder would eat him instead of the bone!

"You're really a most unpleasant dog," he told Thunder. "And your master is a most unpleasant wizard. Shout and Thunder – you're a well-matched couple – but I wish I didn't have to work for you both!"

One day everything went wrong. Oh-Dear-Me burnt the bacon at breakfast, and spilt hot coffee over Mr Shout's foot. He backed away hurriedly from the angry wizard and fell over Thunder's tail. Thunder growled so loudly that Oh-Dear-Me locked himself in the larder.

"Come out!" shouted the wizard. "If you don't, I'll blow a spell through the key-hole and turn you into a jam tart on the dish."

"Oh dear me, don't do that, you might offer me to one of your friends at tea-time!" said the scared brownie, and he came out of the larder in a hurry.

He was sent to get some strange things for some new magic – a ladybird with thirteen spots – a toadstool with two heads – one brown whisker from a mouse – two prickles from a hedgehog – and one hundred whiskers from gooseberries growing on a bush in the kitchen garden.

Oh-Dear-Me was so flustered that he made a lot of mistakes. He brought back a toadstool with two stalks instead of two heads; he found a ladybird with eleven spots, but he counted wrongly and made them thirteen; he brought a yellow mouse-whisker instead of a brown one; and he picked one hundred prickles from the gooseberry bush, instead of one hundred little whiskery hairs from the gooseberries – and he asked the hedgehog for two of his whiskers instead of two prickles.

He hurried back with everything and found the wizard drawing his usual chalk circle in which to do his magic.

"You're late – I've been waiting a long time for you!" shouted the wizard. "Now then – empty all those things into my pot – and *HURRY!*" Poor Oh-Dear-Me shook everything into the steaming pot and the wizard stepped into the circle of chalk and stirred them all together.

"What are you making today, O Master?" asked Oh-Dear-Me, anxiously. "Not a dragon again, I hope? I really do not like dragons prancing round the place. The last one kept sniffing at me as if I were a biscuit or something."

"Be quiet!" bellowed Mr Shout. "I'm

making a new spell, but I shan't tell you what it is."

Oh-Dear-Me stood outside the circle, trembling. Once a thunderstorm had come out of the pot. Suppose another came? Would he have time to hide under the table?

BANG! BONG! BANG!

Green smoke billowed out of the pot, and loud explosions shook it. The wizard peered in, surprised. This wasn't at all how the spell should behave. A spire of green smoke billowed into his face, and he stepped back in alarm.

Oh-Dear-Me gave a shriek. "Master, you've gone green! Your face is as green as grass in the springtime! Oh dear me, whatever's happened? You do look funny. Ha-hah-ha, ho!"

Mr Shout took hold of Oh-Dear-Me and shook him so hard that he rattled. Then he set him down with a bump.

"You gave me the wrong *things*! The spell wasn't right. How *dare* you? I'll turn you into a candle-flame and then I'll blow you out – puff!"

"Oh no, Master!" said poor Oh-Dear-Me, stopping his laughter at once. "Oh please no!"

"Yes, that's what I'll do," said Mr Shout. His dog, Thunder, suddenly barked loudly. Mr Shout turned to him.

"Oh, I forgot that it's your tea-time

and you want your bone. Well, Oh-Dear-Me shall make it for you as usual – and after that – puff! He'll be blown out!"

Oh-Dear-Me began to tremble. Perhaps if he made the dog a very, very nice bone things would be all right. Perhaps Mr Shout was just frightening him. He began to scurry round.

First he got a basin of cool clear water. Then he emptied a little green spell into it and stirred it twenty times. Then he muttered six very magic words, and took two hairs from the dog's tail and dropped them into the water.

"Hurry up!" said the wizard, impatiently. "Why are you always so slow? You're the silliest brownie I've ever known. HURRY UP! I'm getting my biggest puff ready for you."

"It's ready, it's ready!" said Oh-Dear-Me, and picked up the basin. Now all he had to do was to pour it inside the magic circle of chalk and it would turn into a big bone . . .

He ran to the circle – but alas, he tripped over his long beard and fell. The basin shot up into the air – and the magic water spilt all over the wizard.

"Oh dear me – what have I done now?" said the poor little brownie sitting on the floor. "Goodness me – where's Mr Shout?"

The wizard was gone. Not a sign of him was to be seen. But on his chair, where he had been sitting, was a most enormous bone. Oh-Dear-Me stared at it in horror.

"Oh my goodness! Oh dear me! What have I done? The magic water must have gone all over the wizard – and he's been changed into that bone. I must get the bone and change it quickly back into the wizard. Dear, dear – where's the changeback spell? How angry he will be! Oh dear, dear, dear me!"

He reached for the bone – but

somebody got it before him. Thunder the dog snapped at it and held it in his mouth. He growled as if to say, "This is *my* bone! Hands off my bone! I'll bite you if you touch it!"

"Don't crunch it – it's your master!" cried Oh-Dear-Me. "Oh, I must go and get help. Poor Mr Shout!"

He ran into the village to get help – but nobody would go back to Mr Shout's house with Oh-Dear-Me. They laughed loudly.

"What a wonderful thing to happen! He's turned into a bone, and nobody will ever be able to get it away from his horrid dog. Don't interfere, Oh-Dear-Me, or you'll get your head bitten off. It's a very fine punishment for that horrid Mr Shout!"

So it was. His dog won't eat the bone, but he won't let anyone else have it either. Well, you can only say one thing about that, and it's what the little brownie says all day long, OH – DEAR – ME!

## The good old rocking-horse

In the playroom there was a big old rocking-horse. His name was Dobbin, and he was on rockers that went to and fro, to and fro, when anyone rode on him.

He was a dear old horse, and it was very strange that the toys didn't like him! They were afraid of him – and it was all because of something that was quite an accident.

It happened like this.

One day the toy monkey fell off the shelf nearby, and went bump on to the floor. His long tail spread itself out and a bit of it went under one of the rocking-horse's rockers.

Well, that didn't matter a bit – until

John got up on to the horse and rocked to and fro. Then, of course, the rocking-horse pinched the monkey's tail hard every time he rocked over it, and the monkey sobbed and cried after John had gone to bed.

"You great, big, unkind thing!" sobbed the poor monkey, holding his tail between his paws. "You nearly squashed my tail in half. You hurt me dreadfully. I nearly squealed out loud when John was riding you. I don't like you one bit."

"Listen, Monkey," said the rocking-horse in his deep, gentle voice, "I didn't mean to do that. I didn't even know that your tail was there. And in any case I couldn't help it, because John rocked me so hard. But do believe me when I say that I am very, very sorry. I wouldn't have hurt you for the world!"

"I should just think you *are* sorry!" wept the monkey. "Oh, my poor tail! Whatever shall I do with it?"

The teddy bear came up with a

bandage. The baby doll came up with a bowl of water. They bathed the tail and then bound up the squashed end with the bandage. The monkey looked at his tail and felt rather grand when he saw how important it looked with a bandage round it.

It was quite better after a time – but somehow the toys really never forgave the rocking-horse, and he was very sad about it. He knew that he couldn't have helped rocking over the monkey's tail – it was really John's fault for leaving his monkey on the floor – but the toys never seemed to understand that.

So they didn't ask Dobbin to play games with them, and they never even said "yes" when he asked them to have a ride on his back. They just shook their heads and said "no". This hurt the rocking-horse very much, because there was nothing he liked better than giving people rides.

"They think I'm unkind, though I'm not," he thought sadly. "Well, I suppose they will always think the same and I must just put up with it."

Now the toys were very friendly with a little red squirrel who lived in the pine trees at the bottom of the garden. He often used to come leaping up to the windowsill to talk to them. Sometimes he even came right into the playroom and he was delighted one day when they got out one of the dolls' hair brushes and brushed his beautiful bushy tail for him.

"Oh, thank you," he said. "Thank you very much indeed. That's so kind of you. I'll bring you a present one day, Toys."

So when the autumn came he brought them a present. It was two pawsful of nuts! He had picked them from the hazel trees for the toys.

"Here you are," he said. "Nuts for you. They are most delicious! You must crack the hard shell and inside you will find a lovely white nut. I do hope you will like them. Goodbye!"

He sprang off to find some nuts for himself. He meant to hide some in cracks and corners, so that if he awoke in the cold winter days he might find his nuts and have a meal.

The toys looked at the nuts. They were so excited and pleased because they didn't often get any presents. They longed to eat the nuts and see what they tasted like.

The teddy put one into his mouth and tried to crack the shell. But he couldn't. It was much too hard. Then the brown toy dog tried to crack one. But even he couldn't! Then the toys threw the nuts hard on to the floor, but not one cracked.

"We shan't be able to eat the nuts," said the brown dog sadly. "They will be wasted!"

"Let us get the little hammer out of the toy tool-box," said the teddy bear. "Perhaps we can break the nuts with that."

So they looked for the toy hammer and they found it. They put a nut on the floor and hit it hard with the hammer. But the nut jumped away each time, unbroken. It was most tiresome.

Then the rocking-horse spoke up in his deep, gentle voice. "I can crack your nuts for you, Toys! If you will put them underneath my rockers I can rock over them and crack the shells! One of you must ride me to and fro, and then I can easily crack the nuts for you."

The toys all looked at one another. They badly wanted their nuts cracked, so they thought they would do as Dobbin said. They laid all the nuts in a row under his rockers. Then the teddy bear climbed up on the horse's back and began to rock him to and fro.

*Crick-crack, crick-crack* went all the nuts as the shells broke. Inside were the lovely white kernels, so sweet and delicious to eat!

"Thank you, Dobbin!" said the toys. The teddy bear patted him and slid down to get his nuts.

"That was a lovely ride I had!" he whispered to the other toys. "I wouldn't mind another!"

"Have as many as you like!" said Dobbin, who heard what the teddy said. "Are the nuts nice?"

"Delicious! Have one?" said the bear, and he held one up for Dobbin to nibble. "It was kind of you to crack them for us – very friendly indeed."

"I'm such a friendly person," said the rocking-horse sadly, "but you won't make friends with me. I would so much like to give you all a ride."

He looked so sad that the monkey suddenly felt very sorry for him. In a trice he had leapt up on to Dobbin's back.

"Gee-up!" he cried. "I'll be friends with you! Gee-up!"

And then, one after another, all the toys had a ride, and after that they were as friendly as could be. Wasn't it a good thing Dobbin offered to crack their nuts for them?

# *The toys go to the seaside*

Once upon a time the goblin Peeko put his head in at the playroom window and cried, "Who wants a day at the seaside?"

The toys sat up with a jerk. They were all alone in the playroom, for Tom and Beryl, whose toys they were, had gone away to stay at their granny's. The toys were really feeling rather dull. A day at the seaside sounded simply gorgeous!

"How do we go?" asked the pink rabbit.

"By bus," said the goblin, grinning. "*My* bus. I bought it yesterday. Penny each all the way there."

"Oooh!" said the sailor doll, longingly. "I *would* like to see the sea. I've never been there – and it's dreadful to be a sailor doll and not to know what the sea is like, really it is!"

"Come on, then," said Peeko. "Climb out of the window, all of you. There's plenty of room in the bus."

So the pink rabbit, the sailor doll, the yellow duck, the walking doll, the black dog and the blue teddy bear all climbed out of the window and got into the goblin's bus, which was standing on the path outside. The goblin took the wheel. The bus gave a roar and a jolt that sent the pink rabbit nearly through the roof – and it was off!

It was a fine journey to the sea. The goblin knew all the short cuts. It wasn't long before the sailor doll gave a yell and cried, "The sea! The sea!"

"Pooh!" said Peeko. "That's just a rain-puddle."

"Oh," said the sailor doll. But after a bit he shouted again. "The sea! The sea!"

"Pooh!" said the goblin. "That's just a duck-pond."

"But aren't those gulls sailing on it?" asked the doll.

"No, *ducks*!" said Peeko.

"Quack, quack!" said the yellow toy duck, and laughed loudly at the sailor doll. After that the doll didn't say anything at all, not even when they came to the real sea and saw it glittering and shining in the sun. He was afraid it might be a duck-pond too – or an extra big puddle!

They all tumbled out of the bus and ran on to the beach. "I'm off for a swim!" said the yellow duck.

"I'd like a sail in a boat!" said the sailor doll. "Oh! There's a nice little boat over there, just my size."

It belonged to a little boy. He had gone home to dinner and had forgotten to take his boat with him. The sailor doll ran to it, pushed it out to the sea, jumped aboard and was soon off for a fine sail. He *was* enjoying himself!

The pink rabbit thought he would like to make himself a burrow in the sand. It was always so difficult to dig a burrow in the playroom. Now he really would be able to make one! So he began to dig, and showered sand all over the blue teddy bear.

"Hi, hi, Pink Rabbit, what are you doing?" cried the bear. But the pink rabbit was already deep in a sandy tunnel, enjoying himself thoroughly, and didn't hear the bear's shout.

"I shall have a nap," said the blue teddy bear. "Don't disturb me, anybody."

He lay down on the soft yellow sand and shut his eyes. Soon a deep growly snore was heard. The black dog giggled and looked at the walking-doll. "Shall we bury him in sand?" he wuffed. "He would be so surprised when he woke up and found himself a sandy bear."

"Yes, let's," said the doll. So they began to bury the sleeping teddy in sand. They piled it over his legs, they piled it over his fat little tummy, they piled it over his arms. They didn't put any on his head, so all that could be seen of the bear was just his blunt blue nose sticking up. He did look funny.

"I'm off for a walk," said the walking-doll. "This beach is a good place to stretch my legs. I never can walk very far in the playroom – only round and round and round."

She set off over the beach, her long legs twinkling in and out.

The black dog was alone. What should he do?

"The sailor doll is sailing. The yellow duck is swimming. The pink rabbit is burrowing. The teddy bear is sleeping. The walking-doll is walking. I think I will go and sniff round for a big fat bone," said the black dog. So off he went.

Now when Peeko the goblin came on to the beach two or three hours later, to tell the toys that it was time to go home, do you think he could see a single one? No! There didn't seem to be anyone in sight at all! Peeko was annoyed.

"Just like them to disappear when it's time to go home," he said crossly. "Well, I suppose I must just wait for them, that's all. I'll sit down."

Peeko looked for a nice place to sit. He saw a soft-looking humpy bit of sand. It was really the teddy bear's tummy, buried in sand, but he didn't know that. He walked over to the humpy bit and sat right down in the middle of it.

The blue bear woke up with a jump.

"Oooourrrrrr," he growled, and sat up suddenly. The goblin fell over in a fright. The bear snapped at him and growled again. Then he saw it was Peeko.

"What do you mean by sitting down in the middle of me like that?" he said crossly.

"How should I know it was the middle of you when you were all buried in sand?" said Peeko.

"I wasn't," said the bear, in surprise, for he had no idea he had been buried.

"You were," said Peeko. "Just tell me this, Teddy — where in the world has everyone gone to? It's time to go home."

"Is it really?" said the bear, astonished. "Dear me, it seems as if we've only just come!"

"I don't see why you wanted to come at all if all you do is snore," said Peeko. "Waste of a penny, I call it!"

"Well, if you think that, I won't give you my penny," said the teddy, at once.

"Don't be silly," said the goblin. "Look here, Bear, if we don't start soon, it will be too late. What am I to do? I'd better go without you."

"Oh no, don't do that," said the bear in alarm. "I'll soon get the others back. We have a special whistle that we use when it's time to go home."

He pursed up his teddy-bear mouth and whistled. It was a shrill, loud whistle, and every one of the toys heard it. You should have seen them rushing back to the beach!

The sailor doll sailed his ship proudly to shore, jumped out, and pulled the ship on to the sand. He really did feel like a sailor now!

The yellow duck came quacking and swimming in, bobbing up and down in delight. She waddled up the beach, and shook her feathers, sending a shower of drops all over Peeko, who was most annoyed.

The walking-doll tore back across the beach. The black dog came running up, carrying an enormous bone in his mouth, very old and smelly. The toys looked at it in disgust.

"Where's the pink rabbit?" asked Peeko. "He *would* be last!"

The toys giggled. Peeko was standing just at the entrance of the pink rabbit's burrow, but he didn't know he was! The toys knew what would happen – and it did!

The pink rabbit had heard the bear's whistling. He was coming back along his burrow. He suddenly shot out, all legs and sand – and Peeko felt his legs bumped hard, and he sat down very suddenly! The pink rabbit had come out in a great hurry just between the goblin's legs. The toys laughed till they cried. Peeko was quite angry.

"First I sit on a hump that isn't a

hump and get a dreadful fright!" he said. "And then I get bowled over by a silly rabbit who comes out of the sand. Get into the bus all of you, before I say I won't take you home."

They all got into the bus. Most of them were tired and sleepy now, all except the teddy bear, who was very lively indeed – but then, he had been asleep all the time!

They climbed in at the playroom window. They each gave Peeko a penny, and he drove his bus away quietly and parked it under the lilac bush. The toys crept into the cupboard and sat as still as could be.

And when Tom and Beryl came back the next day from their granny's, they *were* surprised to see how well and brown their toys all looked.

"Just as if they had been to the seaside!" said Tom.

"Don't be silly, Tom!" said Beryl.

But he wasn't silly! They *had* been to the seaside!

# *The clown's little trick*

In John's playroom were all kinds of toys, from the big rocking-horse down to the tiny clockwork mouse. They lived together happily and were kind and good to one another, just as John was kind to them.

But one day the fat little toy elephant wasn't so good after all. John had some little chocolate sweets and he seemed to enjoy eating them very much. The toy elephant watched him and wished he could taste one.

"Don't eat any more, John," said his mother. "You must make them last all the week – three a day, I should think."

John put them away on the bottom shelf of his little bookcase. The toy elephant saw exactly where he put them. And that night, in the dark, he left the toy cupboard, walked across the strip of lino, over the carpet, to the little bookcase. He felt about with his trunk and found the paper bag.

He put his trunk inside and felt the

little chocolates there. He got hold of one with his trunk and popped it into his mouth.

"My – it's good!" he whispered to himself. "Very, very good. I like it. Tomorrow night I'll fetch another."

He went back to the toy cupboard, stood himself in a corner and finished eating the sweet. All night long he tasted the flavour of it, and was happy. He didn't think how naughty he had been to take it.

The next night he did the same, putting his little trunk into the bag and pulling out a sweet. He ate it, and then he took another. Nobody saw him. He just stood there in the dark and enjoyed himself.

But John soon found that someone was taking his sweets. He looked sternly at his toys.

"Toys," he said, "it's very sad, but *one* of you is taking my sweets at night. Don't do it. It's very, very wrong."

The toys were dreadfully upset. They

looked at one another when John had gone out for a walk.

"Can one of us be so horrid?" they said. "Who is it? Let him own up at once!"

But the fat little elephant said nothing. He didn't even go red. He wasn't a bit ashamed of himself. And that night he crept off to the paper bag and took two more sweets! He really did.

John was very sad the next day. He looked at the teddy bear, the clockwork clown, the mouse, the monkey, the elephant, the pink cat, the black dog and all the rest of them.

"If it happens again I am afraid I shall have to lock the toy cupboard door, so that none of you can get out at night," he said.

This was a horrid threat. The toys did so love to get out of the cupboard and play around sometimes when John was in bed. When the moon shone in at the window they often had a dance. It would be dreadful if John really did lock the cupboard.

When John had gone out of the room the clockwork clown stood up. "We simply *must* find out who is the thief," he said. "I am not going to let us *all* be punished for something that only *one* of us does! Let that one own up now before it is too late. For I warn him, I shall find him out."

The toy elephant didn't say a word. The clown frowned. "Very well," he said. "It will be very, very bad for the thief when I find him out."

Now, that night the clown did a funny thing. He crept into the larder and found the pot of honey there. He dipped in a paint-brush and hurried down to the floor again. He carefully painted the bit of shiny lino outside the toy cupboard with the honey on the brush. It made it very sticky indeed.

Then the clown went to the breadboard in the playroom cupboard and collected all the crumbs he found there. He took them to the little bookcase and scattered them just in front of the place where the paper sweet bag was kept.

Then he hurried back to the toy cupboard and sat down beside the teddy bear. He didn't tell anyone at all what he had done.

The toys were tired that night. John had played with them a lot that day. They fell asleep and slept soundly, all but the fat little elephant, who was waiting to go and get another sweet. When he was sure everyone was asleep, he crept out of the cupboard as usual. His four feet stepped on the honey. Then, with sticky feet, he padded over to the bookcase and put out his trunk to the sweet bag.

He trod on the scattered crumbs. They stuck to his feet, but he didn't know it. He took a sweet and padded back to the toy cupboard. He spent a long time enjoying the little chocolate.

Now, just at dawn, when a silvery light was coming in through the window, the clockwork clown woke all the toys up.

"Wake up," he said, and his voice sounded so stern that the toys were alarmed.

"What's the matter?" they said.

"I am going to show you who the thief is," said the clown. "I myself don't know who it is yet, but I soon *shall* know! Everyone sit down, please, and show me the soles of your feet!"

In great surprise all the toys did as they were told, and the clown looked at their feet quickly. And, of course, when he came to the elephant's feet, he saw the little crumbs sticking there, and smelt the honey on them, too!

"Here is the thief!" he cried. "Bad little elephant! Look, toys, he has crumbs stuck to his feet! You see, I spread honey just outside the cupboard, and scattered crumbs in front of the bookcase! And the elephant walked over the honey and the crumbs stuck to his feet! So now we know who the thief is! Bad little elephant!"

The toys were angry with the elephant. They turned him out of the toy cupboard. They made him go and stand in front of the sweet bag, so that John would know who the thief was, when he came in.

And he did, of course. "So *you* were the bad little thief!" he said. "I'm ashamed of you. I won't play with you any more!"

And the fat little elephant cried tears into the brick-box at the back of the toy cupboard, and made quite a puddle there.

"Serves you right," said the clown. "We shan't play with you either for a night or two. Perhaps you will think twice the next time you want to take things that don't belong to you!"

It was a clever trick of the clown's, wasn't it?

## Brer Rabbit buys some boots

Now one day it happened that when Brer Rabbit was at the market, he came to the old clothes stall. He had a good look round it, because he badly wanted an old coat for gardening.

There wasn't a coat that fitted him but something else caught his eye – a most *enormous* pair of boots. Brer Rabbit stared at them.

"Who used to wear those?" he asked Brer Possum, who kept the stall.

"Oh, they once belonged to Mr Lion," said Brer Possum. "But he said they hurt his feet, so he sold them to me. No good trying them on, Brer Rabbit – they're ten sizes too large for you!"

"Yes – I know that," said Brer Rabbit. "All the same, I'll have them. Here's the money. Tie them together for me and I'll carry them home round my neck."

So away he went with the enormous boots. He grinned as he went. Maybe they wouldn't fit him – but he would find them mighty useful, all the same!

Now in those days Brer Wolf was making himself a great nuisance. He was a very hungry fellow, and he was always sniffing after Brer Rabbit and Brer Coon and even Brer Terrapin. They were getting very tired of him indeed.

Brer Terrapin told Brer Rabbit to be careful at night and lock and bolt his door and windows. Brer Rabbit nodded. "I'll do that," he said. "But I'm going to scare old Brer Wolf so much that he'll soon begin locking *his* doors and windows!"

"It'll take a lot to make Brer Wolf do *that*," said Brer Terrapin. "Ah, he's a wily fellow is Brer Wolf, and a mighty strong one, too."

Now one night it began to rain, and it rained all the next day and the next one, too. Mud was everywhere and the creatures slipped and slithered about whenever they went out. Brer Rabbit had plenty of food in his cupboard so he didn't go out at all. He knew quite well that Brer Wolf was hiding in the bush round the corner. Little Jack Sparrow had sat on his window-sill and told him so!

"He's a-coming to your house tonight, Brer Rabbit," chirruped Jack Sparrow. "I sat in the bush he hid under, and I heard him tell Brer Bear so, when he came lumbering by. So you be careful, Brer Rabbit, you be mighty careful!"

Well, that night, just before it was dark, Brer Rabbit put on the great big boots he had bought at the market. My, how enormous they were on his little feet and legs! He had to tie

294

them on with string to keep them there.

He looked out of his window. Brer Wolf wouldn't come along till it was dark – he could safely go out now. So out he went in the enormous boots, clumping along in the mud. But what a curious thing – he walked *backwards*! Very awkward it was, too, but Brer Rabbit didn't mind. No – he walked backwards to his gate, backwards through it, and backwards in the thick mud down the road. He walked backwards into the wood just there, and then stood still and grinned.

"Now *forwards*, Brer Rabbit!" he said, and off he walked back to his house, treading carefully in the footsteps he had already made.

He went into his house and took off his boots. He locked his doors and his windows, and sat down, listening with both his ears.

Soon he heard someone coming down the muddy lane, growling all the time.

It sounded like old Brer Wolf. Brer Rabbit sat in his armchair and waited.

That was surely Brer Wolf coming through the gate! Brer Rabbit heard it creak. And now he was coming up to the front door. He had a lantern, because Brer Rabbit could see the light through the window.

"Bang-bang!" That was a *very* loud knock on the door. Brer Rabbit grinned, and called out at once.

"Who's there, disturbing me and my friend at this time of night? Go away!"

"It's Brer Wolf!" cried Brer Wolf, and banged at the door again. "Let me in. I've something to talk about with you."

"Well, I've something to talk about with my friend," said Brer Rabbit. "I'm busy. I don't want to see you."

Now Brer Wolf had already noticed the enormous footmarks down the lane, and how they went through Brer Rabbit's gate and up the path to his door. He couldn't *imagine* whose footprints they were. Surely they

couldn't belong to Brer Rabbit's visitor!
What an enormous fellow he must be!

"Who's this friend of yours?" he
called. "He must be pretty big."

"It's Old Man Wolf-Eater," called
back Brer Rabbit. "Can't you hear him
rattling his teeth at the sound of your
voice?"

And Brer Rabbit rattled a tin spoon
inside an empty saucepan! Brer Wolf
was most surprised. He looked down at
the big footprints and frowned.

"I never heard of Old Man Wolf-Eater
in my life," he said.

"Well, come along in and meet him
then," said Brer Rabbit. "I'll open the
door. But be careful of him, Brer Wolf
– he's pretty hungry tonight."

Brer Wolf heard Brer Rabbit's
footsteps coming to the door. "Wait!"
he said. "I don't think I'll disturb you
tonight after all."

"That's all right – you just come along
in!" said Brer Rabbit, pretending to
unlock the front door, and making a

great noise about it. "Just be careful Old Man Wolf-Eater doesn't jump on you, that's all!"

Brer Wolf took one more look at the enormous footprints going up to the front door, and decided to go home at once! He didn't even stop to say goodbye!

Brer Rabbit heard him scuttling away to the front gate and grinned. "Hey, there, Old Man Wolf-Eater!" he said, as he walked back into his cosy kitchen. "Brer Wolf won't even stay to say how-do-you-do!"

But, of course, there was nobody in the kitchen, nobody at all!

"What a rude fellow Brer Wolf is, to be sure!" said Brer Rabbit, sitting down by the fire.

"And what a sly old rascal *you* are, Brer Rabbit!" he added, laughing to himself.

## *She couldn't keep a secret*

It wasn't a bit of good telling anything to Marybelle if you wanted to keep it secret – because Marybelle would at once go round and tell everyone else!

It was most annoying. When Kitty told Marybelle she was making a hanky-case for her friend Lucy, and it was to be a real surprise, what did Marybelle do but go and whisper it into Lucy's ear at once. So it wasn't a surprise after all.

And when Tom mentioned to Marybelle that his mother couldn't give him money that week to buy the toy he wanted, Marybelle ran round and told everyone that Tom's mother was so poor she couldn't even buy him a toy!

That made Tom very angry. He spoke to the others when Marybelle wasn't there. "Can't we stop that silly Marybelle from repeating everything, and sometimes repeating it wrong?" he said. "She really does make such mischief – and she never gets punished for it!"

"Well, it's our own fault for telling her things," said Lucy.

"Yes, but you can't remember not to talk to Marybelle," said Tom. "I can't, anyway."

"I think I know how we could stop her running round and repeating everything," said Ronnie, with a grin.

"How?" asked everyone at once.

"Well," said Ronnie, "we could tell her silly, ridiculous things and beg her not to repeat them in case they aren't true – which they wouldn't be, of course. And then when she *does* go and repeat them everyone will laugh at her. She won't like that."

"What kind of things would we say to

her?" asked Tom.

"Well – I could say, 'Marybelle, have you heard that the postman lost all his letters in the duck-pond yesterday?'" said Ronnie. "And I would say, 'Now, don't tell anyone, because it probably isn't true.' But off she would go, of course, and what a to-do there would be!"

"Yes. That sounds a good idea," said Tom. "We'll do it. You tell her that one about the postman to start with, Ronnie."

So Ronnie did. He waited until he had got Marybelle alone, and then he whispered mysteriously to her, "Marybelle, have you heard that the postman lost all his letters in the duck-pond yesterday? Don't repeat it, for it may not be true."

Marybelle's eyes almost fell out of her head. Gracious! All the letters lost – in the duck-pond too!

She ran off at once. "Did you know that the postman dropped all the letters into the duck-pond yesterday?" she said to everyone she met. "Well, he did!"

Now, the postman's little boy heard that Marybelle was saying this, and he asked his father about it. The postman was most annoyed. He went straight to Marybelle's house to see her mother.

"Will you please stop your little girl from saying that I dropped all the letters into the duck-pond yesterday?" he said. "I am most annoyed about it. I have never lost a letter in my life!"

Poor Marybelle! She had to apologize to the postman. She scolded Ronnie for saying such a thing.

"Well, I told you not to repeat it in case it wasn't true," said Ronnie. "It's your own fault."

Now the next day Tom went up to Marybelle and whispered something to her. "Have you heard that old Mrs Loo, the sweetshop woman, gives peppermints to her hens, and that's why she never has any when we want to buy them?" he said. "Now, don't you repeat that, Marybelle, in case it isn't true."

"Gives peppermints to hens!" cried Marybelle. "The silly old woman! No wonder she has none to sell."

Off ran Marybelle to tell everyone. How they laughed at her behind her back! But somebody happened to tell old Mrs Loo about it and she was very cross. And the next time Marybelle went into her shop for some sweets, she wouldn't sell her any.

"No," she said. "You're the silly girl that says I feed my hens with peppermints. Such a stupid thing to say! I'd make them ill if I did. You go away and buy sweets somewhere else."

Marybelle cried. She went to Tom and told him he was mean to tell her something that wasn't true. "Well, I warned you not to say anything, in case it wasn't true," said Tom. "It is your own fault, Marybelle."

Then Lucy had a turn. She went to Marybelle, looking most mysterious.

"Marybelle! Have you heard that the grocer has a pony he will let children ride up and down the street for a penny? Isn't it exciting? But don't say a word about it, in case it isn't true."

Well, Marybelle loved riding ponies, and she made up her mind to be the first one riding the grocer's. So she took a penny from her money-box and ran to the shop.

"Please," she said to the grocer, "here is my penny. Now let me ride on your pony."

"What pony?" said the grocer.

"*Yours*!" said Marybelle. "I've heard that we can ride it for a penny."

"Don't be silly," said the grocer. "I've got no pony, and I wouldn't let you children ride it if I had. Run away and don't come to me with silly ideas like that."

How everyone laughed at Marybelle! She was very angry with Lucy. "Well, I told you it might not be true," said Lucy. "I did warn you, Marybelle."

Then Jack went to Marybelle, and told her a little story of his own. "Marybelle! Have you heard that Teacher's dog chased Mrs Brown's cat, and bit its tail?" he said. "Now, don't you repeat that, in case it isn't true."

Any bit of news, however silly or small, was enough to set Marybelle's tongue wagging. In a trice she was telling everyone what Jack had said.

"I say, did you know that Teacher's dog chased Mrs Brown's cat and bit its tail? Fancy that! Teacher always says her dog never chases cats."

Now, old Mrs Brown was the great-aunt of one of the children. This child told Mrs Brown what Marybelle had said, and she was full of horror to think that her poor cat had been chased and bitten by the teacher's big dog.

So up she went to the school to complain. "I shall go to the police about it if your dog chases my cat again," she said. "A great big dog like that!"

"But he *never* chases anything!" said the teacher, in surprise. "He's too old. Who told you that, Mrs Brown?"

"My great-niece, young Gladys," said Mrs Brown. So Gladys was sent for, and asked about the tale of the dog and cat.

"Oh, Marybelle told me," said Gladys. "She was telling everyone."

Marybelle was sent for, and was scolded by the teacher for saying such an unkind thing about her poor old dog.

"Jack told me," wept Marybelle.

"It was only a made-up story," said Jack, grinning. "I warned Marybelle not to repeat it in case it wasn't true. But she can't help repeating anything, however silly it is — or however secret. We've been telling her all sorts of silly tales, and she's been repeating them all — and getting into trouble, too!"

Marybelle burst into tears again. "You horrid boy! You've got me into trouble."

"No. You got yourself into trouble," said Jack. "And you always will,

Marybelle. You can't hold your tongue, you see, and you can never keep a secret, even if it belongs to somebody else."

"Then I shan't ever believe anything anyone says!" said Marybelle, angrily.

"Right," said Jack. "Then, maybe, you won't repeat it!"

And now poor Marybelle is in a great fix, because she never knows whether any bit of news is true or made-up. So she doesn't dare to repeat it in case she gets into trouble again.

It's a funny way of learning to keep secrets, isn't it? But it's the only way with Marybelles!

## *Brer Rabbit has a laugh*

N ow once it happened that when carrots were scarce, Brer Wolf had plenty to sell. So everyone went to him to buy a sackful, and Brer Wolf soon began to make a lot of money.

Brer Rabbit didn't go to him till his larder was bare. Then he took a sack and a purse of money and went to Brer Wolf's with the others.

"A sack of carrots, Brer Wolf!" he said, holding out his big sack.

"I've got a sackful ready," said Brer Wolf. "Leave me your empty sack, and take this sackful."

Brer Rabbit peeped in at the top of the full sack. Big, round carrots lay there, red and well-grown.

"Thanks," he said, paid out his money, put the sack on his shoulder and went off.

But what a temper he was in that evening when he opened the sack and emptied out the carrots on the floor of his cellar!

"Only the top ones are good!" he said. "All the ones underneath are bad. I'll go and tell Brer Wolf what I think of him! I'll either have my money back or a sackful of *good* carrots!"

So off he went, and on the way he met old Brer Terrapin. "You look puffed up and fierce," said Brer Terrapin. "You going to fight someone, Brer Rabbit?"

"Yes. I'm after Brer Wolf," said Brer Rabbit. "He sold me a sack of rotten carrots."

"Ah, he had that one ready for you for a long time!" said Brer Terrapin. "Don't go near him, Brer Rabbit. He's waiting for you! You'll find yourself being cooked with some of his carrots if you go shouting outside his door."

Brer Rabbit marched along, fuming. But he stopped outside Brer Wolf's house, instead of marching in, to knock loudly at the door. Nobody was about but, as Brer Rabbit stood there, Mrs Wolf came out with a basket of washing. She set it down and began to hang it out on the line.

"My, my!" said Brer Rabbit. "What fine clothes Brer Wolf does have now, to be sure! He must think a mighty lot of himself!"

"They're all bought out of carrot-money," said Brer Terrapin. "They're his best clothes. He's been asked to dinner with Mr Lion, so he's told his wife to wash them and get them ready for him to wear tomorrow."

"Has he now?" said Brer Rabbit, and stared at the clothes on the line for so long that Brer Terrapin thought he must have gone to sleep on his feet!

"I've got a plan, Brer Terrapin," he said, softly. "And you're in it. Now, you just listen!"

Brer Terrapin listened, with his little head on one side. He laughed loudly. "It's a good plan," he said. "I'll help!"

Now, that night, Brer Rabbit crept into Brer Wolf's garden, where his clothes still flapped on the line, and he unpegged every single one. He pegged up instead a whole row of rotten carrots, and very peculiar they looked, dangling from the line.

Then he crept away to Brer Bear's, and pegged all Brer Wolf's grand clothes on *his* washing-line, one by one! They flapped in the moonlight, a very grand set of clothes indeed!

Brer Terrapin was with him, chuckling away. "Now it's *your* turn to help us along," said Brer Rabbit, as they went home together. "It's no good *me* doing this next bit – Brer Wolf would soon smell a rat! You know what to do and say, don't you, Brer Terrapin?"

"Ay, ay, Captain!" said Brer Terrapin. "I only hope I don't crack my shell with laughing!"

BRER
WOLF

Next morning Brer Terrapin was outside Brer Wolf's back garden, waiting. Soon he heard Mrs Wolf come hurrying out to take in the clothes she had hung out to dry the afternoon before.

She gave a loud scream and then another. "Oh! OH! Where are the clothes, the splendid, wonderful clothes? And what's this pegged up – carrots! CARROTS! Ohhhh!"

Brer Wolf came rushing out. "What's the matter? What's all this noise about? Good gracious, where are my clothes? Who's taken them – and left these carrots? It's Brer Rabbit, I know it is! I'll have his whiskers off! I'll pull his tail out. I'll . . ."

Brer Terrapin popped his head over the wall. "You sound in a grand old temper, Brer Wolf!" he said. "What's biting you?"

"Brer Rabbit's taken my new clothes!" bellowed Brer Wolf. "I guess they're hanging on his line now – or packed away in his chest. I'll pull his ears off, I'll . . ."

"Oh, your new clothes?" said Brer Terrapin, in a surprised kind of voice. "I know where *they* are!"

"You do? Well, tell me then!" said Brer Wolf, with a roar.

"Oh no. They're not at Brer Rabbit's, I'll tell you that," said Brer Terrapin. "But I'm not telling where they are — getting into trouble for nothing!"

"You just tell me!" said Brer Wolf, so angrily that Brer Terrapin put his head back into his shell.

"I'll tell you tomorrow maybe," said Brer Terrapin.

"Tomorrow! Why, I want to wear them today!" said Brer Wolf. "Don't you know I'm going to dinner with Mr Lion?"

"Much I care!" said Brer Terrapin, his head still in his shell. "Nobody's going to shout at *me*! Nobody's going to tell *me* what to do!"

Brer Wolf had to calm down. He

simply *had* to know where his new clothes were. He spoke in a quieter voice so as not to scare Brer Terrapin any more.

"You tell me," he said. "Go on, Brer Terrapin. You tell me and I'll give you a reward."

"What reward?" asked Brer Terrapin at once.

"Well – what do you want?" asked Brer Wolf.

"I'm mighty fond of carrots," said Brer Terrapin. "I'll take a sack of carrots for my reward."

"Oh no you won't," said Brer Wolf.

"Goodbye then," said Brer Terrapin, moving off slowly. "Wear your old clothes to go and see Mr Lion. What do *I* care?"

"Brer Terrapin, wait," cried Brer Wolf. "Here's a sack of carrots, see? You shall have them all if you tell me where my clothes are."

"You empty out the carrots and let me see if they're all good," said Brer

Terrapin. "I don't like the sight of those rotten ones hanging on your line, Brer Wolf. You let me see what's in the sack."

Brer Wolf emptied them out. There were six or seven bad ones and Brer Terrapin made him replace them with good ones.

"Now put the sack on my back," he said, "and I'll be off with it."

"You haven't told me where my clothes are," shouted Brer Wolf, in a panic.

"Oh no. I forgot," said Brer Terrapin. "Well, you go and look in Brer Bear's backyard, Brer Wolf, and you'll see them hanging there on his line. Aha — I reckon old Brer Bear must be going to visit Mr Lion himself, and he wants to be smart. Your clothes will just about fit him."

Brer Wolf gave such a bellow of rage that all the carrots fell off the clothes line. Then he streaked out of the garden and up the lane to the hill where Brer Bear lived with his family.

"Good day, Ma'am," said Brer

Terrapin politely to Mrs Wolf. "I'll be getting along with my sack of carrots."

And off he lumbered down the lane, the sack neatly balanced on his shelly back, humming a jolly little song as he went. He came to Brer Rabbit's house and turned in at the gate. Brer Rabbit ran out to meet him and stored the sack in his cellar at once and locked the door.

"What happened?" he asked, and laughed till the tears ran down his whiskers to hear how Brer Wolf had listened to old Brer Terrapin.

"There'll be mighty fine ructions up at Brer Bear's right now," said Brer Terrapin, cocking his head and listening. "Brer Wolf will see his clothes there, and he'll tell Brer Bear a lot of rude things — and old Brer Bear he'll come running out ready to swing Brer Wolf over the wall and into the river. My, I wish I could hear them!"

Just at that moment there came a great noise down the lane and Brer Wolf appeared, bellowing in fear, with

Brer Bear after him, smacking at him with a pair of fine red trousers, a blue coat and a yellow waistcoat!

"Take that and that!" grunted Brer Bear. "Hanging your silly clothes on my washing-line and then telling me I'd stolen them."

"Don't, don't, they'll soon be nothing but rags!" yelled Brer Wolf.

But Brer Bear didn't care if they were! The two of them disappeared down the lane, bellowing and growling and grunting, and Brer Rabbit began to laugh again.

"Old Brer Bear,
He doesn't care,
If Old Brer Wolf
Has nothing to wear!"

sang Brer Rabbit. "Come on, Brer Terrapin – let's get those carrots and make some soup. Laughing is hungry work!"

"So it is," said Brer Terrapin. "So it is!"

# The magic claws

There was once a gnome called Scruffy who found a magic spell by accident. It was a strange spell that had been lost for a great many years.

It was a spell to make pink claws for witch-cats! Witch-cats were never allowed to have claws, because they were quite powerful enough without wearing strong sharp claws too! So there had been for many years a law in Fairyland that no cat belonging to a witch should wear claws.

The spell to make claws had been buried deep in a wood – and Scruffy had found it by accident, when he was digging up a fern to sell.

He undid the string – and opened the

box he had found – and in it were two pink claws! Scruffy knew what they were at once – the claws that could work the spell to make others like themselves!

Now Scruffy should really have taken the box to the King – but he didn't. He knew he could make a lot of money for himself by selling witch-claws! So he took the box home, and began to practise the spell.

Very soon he had made twenty more pink claws, sharp and strong! Good! He packed them up and went to visit the witches at night. How pleased they were to buy the pink claws for their black cats! Now they would be able to catch rats again!

Scruffy sold all his claws that night. The next day he made twenty more – and sold those too. Goodness knows how many more he would have made and sold if something hadn't happened.

One of the witch-cats, fitted up nicely with strong pink claws, scratched a little pixie hurrying by to market. The pixie ran to the King and showed the long scratch down his little pink arm.

"The witch-cats have claws again, Your Majesty!" he cried. "Someone has found the old spell – and the witches are arming their cats with claws once more! What shall we do?"

"Call out the army!" ordered the King. "Call out the navy too – and the air force as well! I'll find the fairy who has the claw-spell before the day is out!"

So his army of rabbits marched up. His navy of frogs sailed up the stream. His air force of wasps and bees buzzed by in lines. Everything was ready!

Scruffy soon found out what was happening. He was frightened almost out of his life! He knew he would be severely punished if he was found with the claw-spell on him. What could he do?

"I'll run away!" he thought, in dismay. "Even if I throw away the spell, one of the witches will tell. I must go!"

So he packed up his bag and left at once. He ran out of the gates of Fairyland and didn't stop until he sat down under a hedge in our world. He was hot and tired. He was sad and homesick.

Above him were some pink wild roses. They scented the air and made everything sweet. The bush spoke to him.

"Why do you weep, little gnome?"

The gnome told his story, and showed the pink claws that belonged to the spell. The bush waved about in excitement.

"Little gnome, those claws are just what I want! My stems are not strong enough to stand up by themselves, so they have to lean on other bushes, and very often I cannot get high enough to feel the sunshine on me. If only you would give me some of those pink claws to set all the way up my stems, I could use them to climb with – and I would soon be at the top of the bushes, waving about in the sunshine!"

Scruffy was surprised to hear this. He looked closely at the bush. It was quite true, the stems were very weak and could not stand upright by themselves as those of other bushes did.

Scruffy was glad to please anyone, he felt so sad and ashamed. He set to work to make the spell once more.

Under his hands appeared the magic pink claws – one, two, three, four – twelve, fifteen, twenty! There they lay in a little heap, ready to be used. But not for witch-cats this time! No – Scruffy was not going to sell them, he was going to give them away.

He took up the sharp, curved claws. He went to a stem and, pressing a claw into it, he muttered a magic word that made it grow. Hey presto, the claw stayed there! Then Scruffy took up the next pink claw and did the same thing. It grew on the stem in a trice.

All the twenty claws were soon used – and Scruffy had to make some more for the grateful wild rose bush. It was not long before all the stems were neatly set with strong magic claws. The bush was glad. She used them as hooks to help herself climb higher up. Now she would always be able to reach the golden sunshine.

"Thank you, little gnome," she said gratefully. "You are very clever. You have done me a good turn today. Stay here in our world and help my brothers and sisters too!"

Scruffy never went back to Fairyland. He is still here with us, fitting the wild rose stems with pink claws. Have you seen them? Do look! You will find them growing all the way up the stem, strong, curved cats' claws! Pick a few off carefully and make a wish. There may be enough magic in them to make a wish come true. You never know!

# *Nobby's school*

Nobby the gnome has a dear little
    school
For kittens and froggies and rabbits.
He stands by his blackboard out there
    in the wood
And teaches them all kinds of habits.

The froggies learn just how to flick out
    their tongues
To catch any flies that appear,
The rabbits are taught to show bobtails
    of white
As a signal that danger is near!

The kittens learn purring, and mewing
    as well,
And how to put claws out and in —
Really the school is an excellent one,
With *plenty* of prizes to win!

# A tale of the blue-eyed cat

"I wish," said the black cat loudly, "I do wish that the pink rabbit would go to some other toy cupboard to live."

The black cat was a toy cat. She wasn't much bigger than a small kitten, but she was as grown-up as a cat in her ways.

The pink rabbit glared at the toy cat. "And *I* wish," he said, "that silly black cats with blue eyes would go and jump out of the window. *Blue* eyes! Whoever heard of blue eyes for a cat? Cats have green ones."

"Now, now," said the teddy bear. "Don't start squabbling again, you two. You really ought to behave better, Rabbit, because you are much older

than the toy cat."

The pink rabbit scowled. He was dressed very smartly in blue velvet trousers and a red coat. On his coat were three glass buttons, as green as grass. The pink rabbit was very proud of them.

"Look!" he said to the cat, pointing to his gleaming glass buttons. "Why haven't you got eyes as green as my buttons? Fancy having *blue* eyes!"

"Be quiet, Rabbit. She can't help it," said the big doll. "I've got blue eyes, too."

"It's nice in a doll," said the rabbit. "And look at that cat's tail, too – all the hairs have come off at the end!"

"Well, she couldn't help the puppy chewing her tail," said the bear. "Don't be so mean and bad-tempered, Rabbit."

That was the worst of Rabbit. He *was* so mean. If anyone did anything he didn't like, he said mean things and played nasty tricks, too, on anybody who annoyed him. When the bear grumbled at him one day, he hid behind the curtain with a big pin. And as soon as the bear came along, Rabbit pinned him to the curtain so that he couldn't get away. That was the sort of thing he did.

So nobody liked him much, and they all thought him vain and silly.

The black cat disliked him very much. If she could she always turned her back on him, and he didn't like that.

"Stuck-up creature!" he grumbled. "With her silly blue ribbon and great, staring blue eyes."

One day the toy cat found a piece of chocolate dropped on the floor. She was very pleased. She bit it into many small pieces, and gave a bit to all her friends. But she didn't give even a lick to the rabbit.

"Mean thing!" he said, when he saw everyone munching chocolate. "All right; you just wait. I'll pay you back some day, yes, I will!"

Now, the next week, the black cat felt worried. She couldn't see properly out of one of her blue eyes. She told the bear about it and he had a look at the eye.

"Goodness! It's coming loose!" he said. "I hope Mary notices it, Cat, or it may drop off and be lost. You'd look funny with only one eye."

Mary was the little girl in whose

playroom they all lived. The toy cat kept staring at her, hoping she would notice her loose eye. But she didn't.

Mary had just got a new book and she couldn't stop reading it. You know how it is when you have an exciting book. You just want to go on and on reading.

So the toy cat's eye got looser and looser. At last it was hanging by only one thread, and still Mary hadn't noticed it. She was nearly at the end of her book, though, and the cat hoped maybe her eye would hold on till Mary had finished reading. Then she would be sure to notice her toy cat's eye.

But that night, after Mary had gone to bed, the cat's eye dropped right off! She had been sitting quite still, afraid she might jerk it off – and then she had forgotten to keep still and had run across the room to speak to the bear.

She felt her eye falling out. It fell on the floor with a little thud – and then it rolled away under the couch! The cat gave a cry.

"Oh, my eye's gone! It's under the couch. Please get it, somebody!"

The toys all lay down and peeped under the couch. All except the rabbit. *He* wasn't going to bother himself! But suddenly he saw, quite near his foot, something that shone blue. He stared at it. Gracious, it was the toy cat's eye! It must have rolled under the couch and out at the other side, and have come right over to where the rabbit sat looking at a picture book!

He looked at the other toys. They were all lying on the floor, poking about under the couch. The toy cat was watching, crying tears out of her one eye.

Quick as lightning the rabbit put his foot over the blue glass eye. He kicked it into a corner. Then he got up, went to the corner and, without anybody noticing, put the eye into his pocket.

"Now I've got the cat's eye!" he thought. "Good! She won't get it back again, that's certain. I'll pay her back now for all the things she said to me!"

He went over to the toys and pretended to look for the eye with them. But all the time he could feel it in his pocket. He wanted to laugh.

"Perhaps I'd better hide it safely somewhere," he thought suddenly. "If any of the toys found out that I had the eye, I should get into dreadful trouble. They might turn me out of the playroom. Now, where can I put it?"

Well, you will never guess where he hid it! It really was a very clever place. He went into the dolls' house. There was nobody there, for all the dolls were helping the cat to look for her dropped eye.

He went into the kitchen. He lifted up the lid of the tiny kettle set on the toy stove – and he dropped the eye in there. It just went in nicely.

Then he put the lid on and ran out quietly. Nobody would ever, ever find the eye now, because the dolls' house dolls never used that kettle. They had a smaller one they liked better.

The toy cat was very miserable indeed. She cried bitterly. The toys tried to comfort her. Only the pink rabbit didn't say anything nice. He was glad.

"How mean and unkind you are, Rabbit," said everyone.

But he didn't care a bit.

The next day Mary finished her book, and had time to look at her toys again. And, of course, she noticed at once that the toy cat had only one eye. She was very upset.

"You look *dreadful*!" she said. "You must have dropped it. I'll look around for it." But she couldn't find it, of course, because it was in the kettle.

"Whatever shall I do with you?" said Mary to the miserable toy cat. "You can't go about with one eye, that's certain. And I haven't a blue button that would do for you. What *can* I do?"

She looked at all the other toys, and she suddenly saw the pink rabbit, dressed so smartly in his velvet coat and trousers, with the three gleaming green buttons on his coat.

"Oh! Of *course. I* know what to do," cried Mary; and she picked up the surprised rabbit. "You can have *two* new eyes, Toy Cat – proper green ones, this time! I'll take off your old blue one, and put on two of these beautiful green ones. You will look simply lovely!"

Well, what do you think of that? *Snip, snip*, went Mary's scissors, and, to the pink rabbit's horror, the two top buttons of his coat fell off.

Then Mary took off the one blue eye of the toy cat, and put on the two green ones instead. You can't imagine how handsome the cat looked, with two gleaming green eyes, instead of blue ones. She stared round at the toys in delight.

The toy cat looked lovely but the pink rabbit felt cross and unhappy. He had lost his beautiful green buttons and that awful toy cat had got them instead. She was looking at him with his own buttons for eyes. The rabbit could hardly stop himself from crying with rage.

Now, the toys might have been sorry for the rabbit, and tried to comfort him, if something else hadn't happened just then. Mary suddenly decided to give a party for the toy cat to celebrate her beautiful new eyes. And she took the kettle off the toy stove to fill with water so that she might boil it for tea.

And inside she found the blue eye of the toy cat. She picked it out in the very greatest astonishment. She looked at it, and so did all the toys.

"*Who* put that here?" said Mary

Nobody said anything. But something strange happened to the rabbit's pink face. It turned a dark red. Everyone stared at him in surprise, and then they knew who had hidden the blue eye. It was the naughty pink rabbit.

"So *you* hid it," said Mary. "You naughty, mean toy. I suppose you think I'm going to take off the toy

cat's green eyes and give them back to you as buttons now that we have two blue eyes for her again. But I'm not. She can keep her green eyes now. She looks very beautiful with them. As for you, it was a *very good punishment* to lose your lovely buttons. And, what is more, you shan't come to the party."

"Oh, let him come," said the toy cat, so happy now because she had such beautiful green eyes that she simply couldn't be unkind to anyone. "Let him come. I'll forgive him. Give him a chance to be nice."

So he came. But he was very quiet, and sad and well-behaved.

The toys all think he may be better now. But he does feel strange when he sees the toy cat staring at him through the buttons he once wore on his own coat.

# Duffy does his best

Duffy and his sister Dumpy lived together in a dear little house with Paddy the cat. Dumpy was called Dumpy because she was short and plump – but nobody knew why Duffy was called Duffy.

Dumpy kept house for Duffy, and she did it very well. Duffy wasn't really much help. He always got in the way, and he so often forgot the jobs he was meant to do.

"I really don't know what would happen to you, Duffy, if I went away for a holiday," said Dumpy, one day. "You'd forget to do the shopping, you'd never make your bed, and as for the cat I think she'd run away, because

I know you'd never think she was hungry!"

"Really, my dear, you shouldn't say such silly things," said Duffy, quite cross. "I'm quite capable of looking after myself and the house, and Paddy, and I could do it just as well as you do. So there!"

"Well, I'd like to go out this afternoon," said Dumpy. "But there are a few things that must be done, and I'm not sure I can trust you to do them. So I think I won't go out."

"How ridiculous you are!" said Duffy, very much annoyed. "As if I can't remember to do a few things for you! Just tell me what they are and I'll write them down, so that I shall easily remember. And when you come back, my dear, you will find them all done just as well as *you* could do them!"

"All right, Duffy," said Dumpy. "Now listen – there are four things. The first is, I've made a cake. It is over there, cooling. Please put it on a dish and put it on the tea table at half-past four, because I shall bring old Mrs Do-a-Lot home with me and I'd like her to see a nice tea all ready for her. I've laid the table – it just needs the cake on a dish."

"Easy," said Duffy, scribbling down a note in his notebook. "Remember cake."

"The next thing is, please give the cat her dinner when she comes in," said Dumpy. "She's gone off somewhere and she'll be very hungry. Take the fish out of the larder and put it on her dish for her when she comes in."

"Fish on dish," Duffy said and wrote it down carefully. "What next? These things are easy!"

"Well, a boy will come to fetch the kitchen clock," said Dumpy. "It wants mending. Look, I'll stand it here down by the kitchen door, ready for you to give to him. Just hand it out and say it's for Mr Tick-Tock."

"Right," said Duffy, and wrote down 'clock to go away'.

"And the last thing is, could you just put the tea leaves in the dustbin for me when you go into the garden?" said Dumpy. "It's raining at the moment and I don't want to get my feet wet."

"Right," said Duffy again, and wrote quickly in his notebook. " 'Tea leaves'. That will remind me to put them into the dustbin for you. There, my dear, now you can get ready to go out, knowing that all these jobs will be done for you without fail. You needn't worry at all! I can't forget because I've got them all written down!"

"Thank you, Duffy," said Dumpy, and off she went to get ready. Soon she said goodbye and trotted out happily. Duffy waved to her, feeling very good and helpful.

He thought he would like to listen to the radio for a little while. There was a cricket match on somewhere and he liked listening to cricket. His sister Dumpy didn't like it, so he didn't often listen to it. Now he would really enjoy himself!

He turned on the radio, and settled himself down in a chair to listen. He patted the notebook in his pocket. "I've got everything written down. I can't possibly forget," he thought. "As soon as I switch off the radio I will set to work to do everything Dumpy told me."

He listened for a whole hour. Then the cricket was ended so he turned the radio off, got up and stretched himself.

"Very fine cricket," he said. "Now, let me see . . . what did I have to do? I've quite forgotten! Oh dear. Something about that cake over there, I know. Now what did Dumpy tell me about it? Had she made it for somebody? I'll just look and see if there's any cake in the cake tin. If there is she must have made the fresh one for somebody. But who would it be?"

He looked in the cake tin. There was a sponge sandwich there. He scratched his head. "Well now, Dumpy must have meant me to give that cake to someone. What *was* I to do with it?"

He took out his notebook and looked at it. "I've written 'remember cake'," he said. "Well, I've remembered it, but that's about all. Hello – there's somebody at the door."

He went to the door. A small boy was there. He grinned up at Duffy. "I've been sent to collect something," he said.

"Ah! Was it a cake?" asked Duffy at once.

"I wasn't told," said the boy. "But I've brought a basket with me."

"Then it must be the cake," said Duffy, happily. "I'll get it. Half a minute." He took the nicely cooled cake and put it into a paper bag. The boy took it, delighted, and popped it in the basket. "My dad *will* be pleased," he said. "Thank you very much, sir."

"I hope you enjoy it," said Duffy, and shut the door. "Well, that's one thing remembered," he thought to himself.

"Now, what's next on my list of things to do."

He looked at his notebook. " 'Fish on dish'. Ha, fish on dish! Now what does that mean? What dish am I to put it on?"

He saw the empty cake dish on the tea table. Was that the dish for the fish? There didn't seem to be any other dish set ready to be filled. Dumpy must have told him to put the fish on that dish. He went to the larder and looked inside. There was a large cooked herring on an enamel plate. There was no other fish to be seen.

"Well, Herring, you must go on the dish," said Duffy. He took the fish to the tea table and let it slide on to the cake dish. It really looked most peculiar there, and it smelt a bit strong, too.

"Fish on dish. *That's* done," said Duffy, feeling pleased with himself. "Now then, where's my list again? I'm getting on famously. I've remembered the cake and the fish. What's the next thing?"

He read out his next entry. "Clock to go away. Dear me – *clock to go away!* Now, why in the world should the clock go away?"

He looked at the mantelpiece where the clock usually stood, but it wasn't there. Duffy frowned. Now where was the clock gone? He hunted around for it and at last found it standing by the kitchen door. He stared at it.

"Now what are you doing standing by the kitchen door, Clock?" he asked, puzzled. "You are usually on the mantelpiece. Are you ticking? No, you're not. You've stopped. You must be broken. Now why has Dumpy put you by the kitchen door? She usually puts things there when they are to go into the dustbin."

A thought struck him. "Oh yes – now I remember. Dumpy *did* say something about the dustbin. She must have asked me to throw the old broken clock into the dustbin! Well, come along, Clock, into the dustbin you go!"

348

Out he trotted with the kitchen clock, took off the dustbin lid and threw the clock in among the potato peelings and other rubbish.

He went back to the house. Paddy the cat was there, meowing loudly. She rubbed herself against Duffy's legs. "Oh, you've come back, have you?" said Duffy. "Where have you been?"

"Meeow," said the cat, and rubbed herself against Duffy's legs again, almost tripping him up.

"Now, wait a minute," said Duffy, pulling out his notebook again. "I seem to remember Dumpy saying something about you. Maybe you are the fourth thing I had to remember. Just let me look!"

He stared at the fourth thing he had written down. "Tea leaves. *Tea* leaves! – that seems a little peculiar. I'm sure I was to give the cat something to eat, but the only thing left to give it is tea leaves. At least, that's what I've written down. Well, Puss, I suppose it's all right. Maybe you like tea leaves. Cats are curious creatures!"

He found the tea leaves in the sink-basket and emptied them on to the cat's plate. Paddy sniffed at them in surprise. She gave them a small lick and then turned away in disgust.

"Well, well — you can't be very hungry," said Duffy. "Eat them when you feel like it! I'm going to sit down and have a snooze."

So he settled down in his armchair and shut his eyes. He was soon fast asleep. He didn't hear Dumpy come in with old Mrs Do-a-Lot. He didn't see her sniffing the air in surprise. What *was* that fishy smell?

"Oh, Dumpy, dear, do look — somebody has put a herring in your cake dish!" said Mrs Do-a-Lot, suddenly. "What a strange thing to do!"

"Well!" said Dumpy, in astonishment. "That's the herring I told Duffy to put on the cat's dish when she came

meowing for food. Duffy — DUFFY! Wake up at once,"

Duffy woke up. "Hello, Dumpy! How do you do, Mrs Do-a-Lot? I was just having a nap. Dumpy, I remembered to do *everything* you told me to!"

"Oh, *did* you?" said Dumpy. "Well, Duffy, will you please tell me why you put the cat's fish in the middle of the tea table? I didn't tell you to do *that*! Is it supposed to be a joke?"

"My notes said 'fish on dish'," said

Duffy, puzzled. "Look!"

"Duffy, what did you do with the *cake*?" asked Dumpy, looking all round. "I can't see it anywhere. It was the cake I wanted you to put on the cake dish. That's your first note, look, 'remember cake'. Where is it?"

"Oh, dear me – I thought the cake was for the messenger boy who called," said Duffy, shocked. "He said he had been told to collect something and I quite thought it was the cake. He seemed so delighted. He said his dad would be pleased too."

"His dad is the clock-mender, Mr Tick-Tock," said Dumpy, almost in tears. "I expect he *will* be pleased with my beautiful cake. I told you to give the kitchen clock to his boy – it's to be mended. Where's the clock, then?"

"Well, my dear – it was standing over there by the door – and I quite thought it was to go into the dustbin," said poor Duffy.

"You put my lovely kitchen clock into the dustbin! Oh, you wicked fellow!" cried Dumpy, and Mrs Do-a-Lot gave a loud snort of disgust. "I said you were to put the *tea leaves* into the dustbin. Where are your brains, Duffy? Oh dear, oh dear. And now I wonder what you did with the tea leaves?"

"He's put them into the cat's dish," said Mrs Do-a-Lot, with another snort. "Look! No wonder poor Paddy looks disgusted!"

"Well, there wasn't anything left on my notes to give her by the time she came meowing round," said Duffy, desperately. "It's her fault. If she had come right at the beginning of the afternoon I would have had the fish to give her. It's all her fault!"

"Why don't you put *him* into the dustbin?" said Mrs Do-a-Lot.

She looked so fierce that Duffy ran out of the kitchen door and locked himself into the wood shed. He was very sad. He had made all those notes – read them to himself – and had done a whole lot of things. But what was the use? They were all wrong!

Dumpy put her head in at the window. "Duffy, don't be silly. Come back. It's not the cat's fault and it isn't yours either, really. It's mine. I should have known that you would get it all wrong! And, by the way, Mrs Do-a-Lot says she knows why you are called Duffy."

"Oh, she does, does she?" said Duffy. "Well, why then?"

"Because it's short for Duffer!" said Dumpy, with a giggle. "I shan't call you Duffy again. Come on, Duffer, let's give Paddy her fish and then we can have some tea!"

Well, I can't help thinking Mrs Do-a-Lot is right. Poor old Duffer, he couldn't have made a worse muddle if he had tried, could he?

# The lost doll's pram

"Mummy, I do so wish Tibbles wouldn't keep jumping into my doll's pram," said Eileen. "How can I stop her?"

"Well, you could stop her by doing what *I* used to do, when you were a baby in your pram," said Mummy. "You can put a net over the pram so that no cat can jump into it."

"Oh dear – I don't want to do that," said Eileen. "It would be an awful bother to have to do that every time I put my dolls to sleep. I shall shout at Tibbles next time I find her in my doll's pram!"

Eileen found her there the very next morning, curled up under the

eiderdown, fast asleep. Shout! Tibbles
gave a meow of surprise, and leapt out
at once. She was never shouted at by
Eileen and she didn't like it at all.

"You are *not* to get into the pram,"
said Eileen to Tibbles. "I have told you
ever so often. You are a naughty little
cat. Do you want to smother Rosebud
or Josephine, by lying on top of them?
Shoo! Go away!"

Tibbles ran away — but will you
believe it, as soon as Eileen went
indoors again, Tibbles jumped right
into the pram once more!

She did love that pram. It was so soft
inside and so cosy. She loved cuddling
down, curling herself up and going to
sleep in peace and quiet there.

"It just fits me nicely," she thought.
"I can share it with the dolls. They
never seem to mind. They don't even
kick me."

Now the next day three naughty boys
came along with a naughty little girl.
They saw some apples hanging on the

trees in Eileen's garden, and they crept in at the gate to take some.

Eileen saw them from the window. She rushed out into the garden. "You bad children! That's stealing! Go away and leave my daddy's apples alone."

"Give us some!" shouted the biggest boy.

"No, certainly not. If you had come to ask my daddy properly, he would have given you a basketful," cried Eileen. "But people who steal don't get any. Go away!"

"You're a horrid little girl!" shouted the boy. "We'll pay you back!"

And then Eileen's mother came out and the four naughty children ran away. They came peeping over the wall again the day after – but not to take the apples. They meant to pay Eileen back for sending them away.

"Look – there's her doll's pram," whispered the little girl. "Let's take it away into the park and hide it where she can't find it. That will teach her to shout at us and send us away. Quick, Bill – there's no one about – you slip in and get it."

Bill opened the back gate, ran into the garden and took hold of the pram handles. He wheeled the little pram at top speed out of the gate. Slam! – the gate shut, and the four children hurried down the lane to the park.

"She hasn't got any dolls in the pram," said the little girl. "I'd have thrown them into the bushes if she had!"

What a very horrid little girl she was! She had dolls of her own and loved them – and yet she would have done an unkind thing to someone else's dolls! Well, well – some people are strange, aren't they?

The boys stuffed the pram into the middle of a big bush and left it there. Then they went back to Eileen's garden to see what she said when she came out and found her pram missing.

She soon came out with her two dolls, meaning to take them for a walk, as she always did each morning. But where was her pram? It was nowhere to be seen! Eileen looked everywhere for it — and then she saw the four heads of the giggling children, peeping over the wall.

"Have you seen my pram?" she called.

"Yes," they called back.

"Where is it?" shouted Eileen.

"It's hidden in the park where you can't find it!" called the biggest boy. "Ha, ha! You'll never find it again!"

"Mummy, Mummy, come here!" called Eileen, almost in tears. But her mother had just gone next door and she didn't come. So Eileen had to make up her mind herself what she was going to do.

"I must go and look in the park," she thought. "Oh, dear — suppose it rains? My lovely pram will be soaked. Suppose I don't find it? How am I to know where those bad children have put it?"

She put her dolls down just inside the house, ran down the garden again, into the lane and was soon in the park. Now – where should she look?

She hunted here and she hunted there. She looked in this bush and that, but she couldn't find her pram.

"Oh, dear – there are such a lot of bushes and trees!" thought poor Eileen. "I could look all day long and never find my pram. Where *can* it be?"

It was very well hidden indeed. Someone else was well-hidden there too. And that was Tibbles!

Tibbles had been in the pram when the bad children had run off with it, curled up as usual under the eiderdown, fast asleep. When the children had taken the pram, Tibbles had thought it was Eileen taking the dolls for a walk. She hadn't dared to pop her head up, in case Eileen was cross with her. So she just lay there, wondering why the pram went so fast that morning. Then suddenly it was pushed into the bushes, and was still. Tibbles shut her eyes and went to sleep again.

She woke up after a time and stretched herself. Everything seemed very quiet. Tibbles felt hungry and thought she would jump out of the pram and go and find her dinner. She had forgotten that the pram had been taken for a walk – she thought she was still in garden!

She poked her head out from under the covers and looked round. What was this? She was somewhere quite strange! This wasn't her garden. Tibbles sat right up, very frightened.

Where was she? Where was Eileen? What had happened? And dear me, was this rain beginning to fall?

It was. Big drops pattered down on Tibbles, and she crouched down. She hated the rain. She suddenly felt very lonely and frightened and she gave a loud meow.

"MEOW! MEE-OW-EE-OW-EE-OW-EE-OW!"

Nothing happened except that the rain pattered down more loudly. One enormous drop fell splash on to Tibbles' nose, and she meowed angrily.

The rain made a loud noise on the bracken around, and Tibbles couldn't think what it was. She didn't dare to jump out of the pram.

"MEEOW-OW-OW!" she wailed, at the top of her voice.

Eileen was not very far off, and she heard this last MEE-OW. She stopped. That sounded like a cat's voice! Was there a cat lost in the park, caught in the rain that was now pouring down? Poor thing!

"MEEEEEEEEE-OOOW-OOOOW!" wailed Tibbles, and Eileen hurried towards the sound. "MEEE-OW!"

"It seems to come from that bush over there," thought the little girl, and went to it. Another loud wail came from the spot.

"Meee-ow-ow-ow! MEE-ow-ow-OW!"

And then Eileen suddenly saw the handles of her pram sticking out of the bush. How delighted she was! She ran to them and gave a tug – out came her doll's pram – and there, sitting in the middle of it, scared and lonely, was Tibbles!

"Oh, *Tibbles*! It was you I heard meowing!" cried Eileen, in surprise. "You must have been asleep in the pram again when those children ran off with it. Oh, Tibbles, I *am* glad you were in it – it was your meowing that made me find it! I'll never scold you again for getting into the pram!"

She put up the hood, and drew the waterproof cover over Tibbles so that the frightened cat shouldn't get soaked. And then off she went home with her precious pram, not minding the rain in the least because she was so pleased to have found her pram again.

Tibbles couldn't imagine why Eileen made such a fuss of her, but she liked it all the same. The funny thing was that she never, never got into the doll's pram again. She was so afraid it would run off with her into the park and lose her!

So do you know what she does? She gets into the doll's cot up in the playroom and goes to sleep there! I've seen her, and she really does look sweet, curled up with her tail round her nose.

# Tammylin's friend

O nce upon a time there was a little
pixie who didn't like earwigs. Now
this was very silly because earwigs are
clean and tidy creatures and never
mind doing a good turn for the fairies.

Still, Tammylin the pixie couldn't
bear an earwig near her, and whenever
she saw one she always sent it scurrying
away in fright. She kept a little broom
which she used specially for frightening
earwigs, and she often used to sweep
away any that came near her neat little
house and garden.

Now one day when Tammylin was
wandering in the violet wood all by
herself, humming a song and dancing
round the sweet-smelling violets, she

walked quite by mistake into the Green Magician's garden.

He lived in the middle of the wood, and as he had no wall or fence or hedge round his garden, it was very difficult to see it. Tammylin didn't see it at all – and she walked right into it just as the Green Magician was coming out to do his shopping!

"Oho!" he said, and caught hold of Tammylin, who was alarmed and

astonished. "So you've come spying round, have you, to see what kind of secret magic I make? Well, you'll be sorry now! You can be my cook. The rabbit who waited on me has just left to get married – you will do nicely instead."

"I won't, I won't!" squealed Tammylin, and she wriggled as hard as she could. But it wasn't a bit of good. The Green Magician wrapped her up in his green cloak and took her into his cottage. He cut off her pretty silver wings and gave her an apron to wear.

"My wings won't grow for three weeks," sobbed Tammylin. "You are very horrid. I shall run away as soon as you've gone out."

"Oh, no, you won't!" said the Green Magician – and what do you think he did? He took his magic wand, waved it round his garden seven times and called out a magic word – and lo and behold! a great wall grew round it, so high that Tammylin couldn't see the top.

"There," said the magician, pleased. "What do you think of that? You can't escape now."

He went out to do his shopping, unlocking and locking a big door in the wall. Tammylin was left alone to cook the dinner. How she wished she could let her friends know where she was!

When the Green Magician went to market, he heard everyone talking about Tammylin's disappearance, but he didn't say a word. No, he had got a cook for nothing, and he meant to keep her. He went to the fish-stall and bought some herrings. He went to the sweet-stall and bought some peppermints. He went to the fruit-stall and there he bought some pears and a large cauliflower.

He carried them all home in his big bag, and went in through the door in the wall again, locking it after him. He put his shopping down on the kitchen table and told Tammylin to cook the cauliflower for dinner.

"I'm going into the garden to water my flowers," he said. So out he went, and left Tammylin to get on with the cooking. The little pixie sulkily took up the cauliflower – and as she did so, out crept a very large earwig. Tammylin dropped the cauliflower with a shriek.

"Hello, Tammylin," said the earwig in surprise. "How did you come to be here?"

"The Green Magician caught me," said Tammylin, "and I can't escape because there's a high wall round the garden and my wings are cut off. Oh, go away, you horrid earwig! If only you were a butterfly you could fly up over the wall and tell everyone where I am. Then my friends would rescue me. What a pity you are such an ugly, useless earwig."

"You are unkind, Tammylin," said the earwig.

Just then the Green Magician poked his head in at the window. "Who are you talking to?" he said.

"To an earwig, the horrid thing!" said Tammylin.

"Oh, an earwig," said the Magician. "Well, *he's* a prisoner here too – he can crawl around the garden but he can't get out. If it had been a butterfly, a bee, or a moth I'd have stopped him from taking any message to your friends. But an earwig has no wings."

As soon as the magician had gone back to the garden the earwig ran close to Tammylin and began to whisper.

"Listen, Tammylin, the magician is wrong," it said. "I *have* got wings."

Tammylin stared in surprise at the brown, smooth-backed earwig. "You haven't!" she said. "What a storyteller you are!"

"Sh!" said the earwig. "I tell you I *have* got wings. I keep them neatly folded under my back-shell. Look, those brown things on my back are my wing-cases. Watch how I unfold my beautiful gauzy wings."

Tammylin watched in the greatest

astonishment. The earwig lifted up his brown wing-cases from his back and shook out his wings. They were gauzy like a bee's, but long and beautifully folded – just like a fan.

The earwig spread them out. "I'm going off to tell your friends where you are," he said. "They will rescue you soon. Goodbye."

Tammylin watched the earwig fly up into the air on his long gauzy wings, up, up and up – right over the wall. The Green Magician never even saw him.

"Well," thought Tammylin, washing the cauliflower, "I never knew before that earwigs had wings folded so beautifully under their back-shells. How kind of him to fly off to tell my friends. I wish I hadn't been so horrid to earwigs. I never will be again!"

The earwig flew straight to the market-place, folded his wings neatly, poked them tidily under his back-shell with his pincers, and then told everyone where he had seen Tammylin. It wasn't long before the King himself, at the head of twenty men, was riding through the violet wood to rescue Tammylin. But as soon as the Magician heard his King's voice he took down the wall, and fled away to the borders of Fairyland. He knew that it was forbidden to capture pixies.

"But how, how, *how* did the King know where Tammylin was?" he wondered a hundred times a day. He never knew – but Tammylin did not forget her kind friend.

"I will never chase earwigs away again," she said. "I didn't know they were so kind, and had such lovely wings, folded like fans."

"Oh, earwigs are good people," said the King, as she rode back safely with him. "They look after their little ones as few insects do – they are very good mothers. You should not be unkind to anything, Tammylin. Goodness and loveliness may be found in even the ugliest creatures. You never know!"

Now Tammylin is friends with all the earwigs, beetles and spiders that she knows, and never dreams of using her broom to sweep them away. Wasn't it a good thing for her that an earwig had wings! Did *you* know that?

## *She couldn't remember*

"Winnie, you've left the door open again!" called Mummy.

"Bother!" said Winnie, and came back to shut it. "I wish I could remember. I'm always forgetting."

"You should try a little harder to remember," said Mummy. "Goodbye, dear. Hurry, or you'll be late for school."

Winnie banged the front door and ran to the gate. She opened it – and forgot to shut it. Mother knocked on the window.

"Winnie! Winnie! Shut the gate! The dogs will come in and spoil the garden."

But Winnie didn't hear. She was halfway down the road. She really was dreadful about forgetting to shut doors and gates. She just couldn't remember!

She ran to school. She was rather late, so she quickly changed her shoes in the cloakroom and then slipped into her classroom to take her place.

Of course she left the door open! "Do shut the door, Winnie!" said Miss Brown. "One of these days you'll forget to shut a door or a gate, and you'll be very sorry indeed!"

Of course Winnie didn't believe that! It was the sort of thing that grown-ups always said. But wait a minute, Winnie. This time Miss Brown is right – you'll be very sorry indeed next time you leave a door or a gate open!

On the next Saturday Winnie was very pleased because her Auntie Alice had asked her to go to tea. She loved going to Auntie Alice's cottage. It was in the country, and there were plenty of flowers and fruit trees in the garden. Sometimes it was strawberry-time, sometimes there were raspberries to pick, and there were plums, apples and pears later in the year.

"It's apple and pear time now," thought Winnie, as she got ready to go. "Auntie will let me pick plenty, I know, and she'll tell me to take a bagful home. What fun!"

"Winnie, put on your new blue hat!" called Mummy. "Auntie will like to see that. And take your blue scarf too, and your blue handkerchief. Then you will look very nice."

"Ooh, yes!" said Winnie, delighted. So she put on her new blue straw hat with the white daisies round it, and put her blue scarf round her neck. She stuffed her blue handkerchief into her pocket, leaving one end out to show a little. She really did look nice!

Off she went. Auntie Alice was delighted to see her. "You can go to that red apple tree and pick two nice ripe apples to eat," she said to Winnie.

As Winnie was going to the red apple tree, she noticed that all the Michaelmas Daisy plants nearby were cut down before they had even flowered.

"Oh, Auntie, why have you cut them down?" she asked, in disappointment. "I was so looking forward to seeing them all in flower!"

"Well, darling, you left the gate open last time you went home, after seeing me," said Auntie sadly. "And two cows got into the garden and trampled down all my lovely daisies. So we had to cut down the poor broken stalks."

"Oh, Auntie, I'm so sorry," said Winnie, ashamed of herself.

"I think that until something punishes you hard for leaving gates open, you will never remember," said Auntie. "Just see if you can be a good, thoughtful girl today and shut every gate you go through! It is very important in the country."

Well, Winnie remembered to shut the orchard gate. She remembered to shut the field gate when she went through it to look for blackberries. She remembered to shut them both when she came back too. She felt quite

pleased with herself.

But do you know what she didn't do, when she went in to tea? She quite forgot to shut the garden gate that led into the lane! Outside in the lane were two old goats belonging to Mrs Brown up the road. They were always on the look-out for open gates, because they loved eating the flowers and vegetables in a garden – they tasted much nicer than grass in the lane!

When Auntie called Winnie in to tea, the little girl was pleased, for she was very hungry. She had been sitting reading a new story book that Auntie had given her. On the grass beside her were two more books, her new hat, her blue scarf, her handkerchief, and a big bagful of ripe apples.

She jumped up, leaving everything neatly together, and ran into the house. And whilst Winnie was having *her* tea, those two goats came in at the open gate and had *their* tea!

And what do you think they ate for their tea? They ate one new hat, one blue scarf, one blue handkerchief, three story books, twenty-two ripe apples, *and* the bag they were in!

Goats will eat anything – but this was a wonderful tea for them. How they enjoyed it! Nobody knew anything about it till Winnie looked out of the window and saw one of the goats walking about on the lawn, with a bit of her blue scarf hanging out of its mouth. It was just finishing a good chew.

"Oh!" screamed poor Winnie. "Look! That goat is eating my scarf! Quick, Auntie, stop him!"

They rushed out – but it was too late to stop the goats. Everything was inside them! Auntie Alice shooed them angrily away, and then turned to comfort poor Winnie, who was sobbing bitterly.

"They've eaten my new hat with the daisies," sobbed Winnie, "and my scarf and hanky, and my new books, and all my apples! And I haven't time to pick any more because it is time for the bus. Mother will be so cross about my hat! Oh, those horrid, horrid goats! How did they get in?"

"Winnie," said Auntie, in a grave sort of voice, "they got in through the open gate – but who left the gate open?"

Winnie sobbed even more loudly. "I did!" she wept. "It's my own fault. But oh, don't scold me any more because I am so unhappy!"

So Auntie said no more, but took poor Winnie to the bus and put her in, still crying. Mummy wondered whatever the matter was when she saw her little girl coming home with red eyes and tear-stained cheeks.

Winnie soon told her everything. Mummy wasn't cross. She just said, "Well, Winnie, I knew this sort of thing would happen sooner or later. I can't afford to buy you a new hat or scarf. You must wear your old ones again. It's a good thing I haven't given them away."

So Winnie is wearing her old hat and scarf again now, and she feels very sad when she sees all the other children wearing their new ones. When she sees them she frowns and says to herself, "I will always remember to shut doors and gates behind me." And I rather think she will now, don't you?